# WHERE THE SUN GOES TO DIE

## A JONATHAN CROWLEY COLLECTION

I0618514

# JAMES A. MOORE

# Acknowledgments

For Christopher Golden, Tessa Moore, The Necon Family, Brian Keene and the many, many people who have helped me through such troubling times. Also for Joe Lansdale, who reminded me that I love a good western.

# Contents

# The Black Train Blues

**Winter, 1867, Utah**

The wind roared down from the northern slopes and across the plains, bringing stinging ice and grit with it. There was shelter, of course, for anyone who had the money or was working for the railroads. Anyone else was going to be begging. The sun had set and the coolies were done laboring for the day. Several hundred men were gathered together and eating in the long tents set up for just that reason. A few would likely end up moving over to the small town of Coal Pit soon enough, but for the moment they were eating free food and recovering from the vicious weather.

There were nights when the stars shone down and the land around them was beautiful, and then there were times, like the night they were experiencing, when the clouds hid the stars and the moon and left little but darkness and the occasional lantern to show anyone the way to another spot.

In the darkness outside the few sentries sat huddled in their coats, often covered with additional blankets for shelter from the hellish winds, and stared out into the night, looking for signs that the Apache might be coming around to cause mayhem again. Apache? Maybe it was the Navajo. None of the guards knew or much cared as long as the red men stayed away. That was the only good thing about the winter storms; they kept the Indians away.

The storms and the savages were problems, but there were worse things on the minds of the men in charge. They had bigger problems, concerns that put the inconvenience of ice on their supplies to shame and made the Indians seem more like the sort of problem that could be managed with a little extra effort. The Pinkertons had failed them already, and the Pinkertons damned near never failed.

Bram Whittaker shook his head and did his best to remain patient as the telegrapher sent his communication out again. The ticks and clicks of the telegraph device made no sense to the foreman, but he knew from experience that Dan Latham would get the job done. He just didn't want to wait for a response. Four men had died in the last week, and they were dealing with even the Chinamen looking around and considering moving on. Hell, nothing seemed to scare the Chinese, but this was different. This wasn't natural.

Latham looked up from his task and nodded. "It's done. Nothing to do now but wait."

"How long does it take for a telegram to get to someone, Latham?"

"The communication is almost instant." The man shrugged. "The real problem is how long it might take for the man you want to hear from to get the message from the offices I sent it to."

"Any ideas on how long that might be?"

Latham stared at him for a moment and he could see that the man wanted to make a snide comment but was stopping himself. There was no way to know, of course, because there was no way to be sure if Jonathan Crowley was in any of the towns where he'd sent the messages.

In the distance, well beyond where the workers were camped and past even the hell on wheels gatherings in the town of Coal Pit, the winds continued their almost perpetual moans of frozen agony.

And even further away than that, the sound they'd come to dread started up again, a low, mournful bellow that slowly grew in volume and roared toward them along the path they'd been carving across the country.

---

Jonathan Crowley didn't arrive by wagon and he didn't come into town alone. He came on horseback, his lean body settled comfortably in the saddle of a large roan that seemed perfectly content to work its way into the town at a casual speed. The man riding with him was an unpleasant sight, with deathly pale skin and possibly the gauntest features anyone could remember setting eyes on. The few sentries who saw them reported quickly that two riders were coming. Once they realized they weren't red men, they were allowed to come into the town proper.

The cold, impossible though it seemed, had actually grown more intense. The winds cutting across the landscape howled occasionally and merely whistled at other times, but either way they brought with them the sort of chill that cuts into exposed flesh. Crowley seemed not to much care.

The man himself looked around without moving his head much, his face half hidden in the shadows of the wide-brimmed gambler's hat he sported. The expression on his face was mostly neutral, but his eyes spoke of a need to cause somebody bodily harm.

The man with him was dressed in rawhide and wearing a coat that looked to be made of bearskin. His face was lost under a hat that seemed far too fancy for his attire, but his expression made it clear he didn't much care what anyone thought about his clothing.

"You need anything else from me for now?" Slate's voice was exactly as cheerful as his disposition.

Crowley looked at the man and shook his head. "Look around for a bit. Have some fun. Ask a few questions if you have a mind to. I'll talk with you after my meeting."

"I didn't know better, I'd think you were ashamed to be seen with me."

"I was ashamed to be seen with you, I wouldn't be seen with you."

Slate allowed himself a small chuckle and turned his horse toward the obvious center of sin in the area. Crowley continued on alone, his eyes watching each person that he passed.

Most of the people in Coal Pit couldn't have cared less. They had their own troubles and few of them looked like another stranger would impact them one way or the other. The place was a dump at best, with heavy ice on most of the paths that had been mud when the buildings were slapped together. No one living in the place expected to be there for too long. They were there to serve the railroad workers and the only workers who were likely to stay in the area were the ones who had the misfortune of dying there. Death and working on the lines often went hand in hand.

No one much cared for the dead these days. The living had enough troubles of their own.

Crowley stopped in front of the telegraph office. His stay there lasted exactly long enough to know where he had to go to find Abraham Whittaker. One look at his face and the telegraph operator was glad to point him in the right direction.

He rode past the gambling houses, the tents where a few coins bought an escape into opium dreams, and past the clapboard establishments that sold liquor and women, both of dubious nature. None of them mattered to him. He had no desire for escape from his reality. He had plans that required his mind be sharp, though there had been times when he preferred to escape from clarity any way he could.

The foreman for the railroad was settled in his wagon, a great wooden affair that looked far better built than most of the buildings in town. To be fair, it *was* better built, crafted by capable hands and assembled from well-seasoned wood instead of lumber that had barely been planed down to shape by people with little or no knowledge of what they were doing. The differences between craftsmanship and desperation were many.

Bram Whittaker took one look at Crowley and smiled as he rose from his seat behind the narrow desk where he did most of his work. "Is that really you, Jonathan?"

The man stared at him for a second and nodded brusquely. He did not seem nearly as pleased as Whittaker felt.

"To look at you, you've barely aged."

Crowley walked into the office proper and closed the door, soaking in the warmth offered by the stove in the corner. The cold outside was damned near a living thing. "I have always been…lucky with that."

"I sent several telegrams. I had no idea where to find you."

Crowley took off his hat and the thick oilskin duster that covered his frame, and dropped them across one of the three chairs near the desk. "I preferred it that way, Bram. I don't like being found."

"I know, but you always said that if I had another problem, I should let you know. I should ask for your help." The man made no response, and he sighed before he continued. "Jonathan, it's killing my people."

Crowley snorted. "Your people? Three Chinese laborers. Two ex-slaves. Your people?"

"They work for me, Jonathan. They need protection."

"When did you start caring about the lives of others, Bram? When did that happen? You didn't much seem to mind when Bragg got his heart cut out." His eyes cut almost as sharply as his words. "I don't recall you shedding any tears when Loraine Haliwell was screaming for mercy and dying in the middle of the night." Crowley's gaze pinned him in place and Whittaker nearly groaned.

"I was a foolish young man, Jonathan. I was vain and I thought the world was better without their likes in it, but I never did them any harm myself."

Crowley's thin lips pursed for a moment and then broke into the narrow grin that had made more than one man take a step back from him. "I once watched a man drown. He couldn't swim and I could have thrown him a rope and he could have pulled himself back to the ship. I could have gone in after him. I could have told the captain and crew that a man had fallen overboard and they'd have surely gone back for him. I did none of those things. I could have saved him and I chose not to." Crowley walked toward him slowly, his gaze drilling into Whittaker's eyes. "I could have saved him and I didn't. I did not cause his death, but you can believe I caused him harm."

Whittaker stepped back until the wall of his cabin forced him to a stop.

"Why?" Whittaker's voice broke. "Why would you do that?"

Crowley smiled. It has been said, and not without a certain degree of truth, that Crowley's smile is an unpleasant experience for most. Whittaker flinched, forced to remember very abruptly why it was that he'd dreaded the idea of asking the man for assistance. "He deserved his death. That's not the point here. You never lifted a finger against Robert Bragg or Loraine Haliwell, but don't for a moment think you never caused them any harm. You could have saved them a dozen times over and you didn't. Remember that."

Crowley stepped back and settled into one of the two remaining free chairs. Whittaker thought for a long moment and then finally dared taking a seat himself.

"Tell me why you called me here. Why you are asking for my help." Crowley's hands steepled together in front of his chin and he stared with that furious, haunting gaze of his.

"Something out there is killing my people." He shook his head. "The workers, then. It's killing the workers. I have production to keep up, of course but it's more than that. They don't deserve to die that way. Nothing does. Nothing could." He shivered.

Crowley said nothing, but that damned smile of his crept around the corners of his mouth and Whittaker shivered again, despite the warmth within his offices. "Tell me a story, Bram. Make it interesting."

Whittaker reached to the edge of his desk and grabbed for two clean glasses set near a decanter. The whiskey was good, brought with him from Boston when he came to the area. He offered up a glass to Crowley. The man did not turn it down. "It started just a few weeks ago. We've been very fortunate, we've had a few setbacks, but nothing crippling. I mean, Sorensen and his team ran across Indians and got themselves killed a while back. I had to take over for them and I was glad of the work, but I was also terrified. I'm not…I'm not the bravest man, Crowley. You already know that about me. I'm not exactly a coward, but I'm not the bravest of men, either. I have my flaws. We all do."

He stopped long enough to drink a mouthful of the whiskey and to draw in a breath afterward.

"Just the same, I took over the line here and I've done a good job. Production is up. The workers seem happy enough. We've had fewer accidents since I took over. But then last month we ran into something unusual. Last month the train showed itself on the tracks."

"A train?" Crowley's smile twitched.

"Yes, you heard me correctly. A train. The tracks are barely even laid out here. Hell, we're laying them ourselves. It's what we're supposed to do. It's what we're being paid for." His voice broke and Whittaker shook his head and took back another swallow of whiskey. "We've got miles and miles to go before an engine should be anywhere around these rails, but as God is my witness, Jonathan, I have seen the train with my own eyes. A great black engine and a dozen cars behind it. I have seen trains, Jonathan, I know them well. I've been on them and I've watched enough of the rails getting laid down to hear the sound of hammers driving spikes in my sleep. But I have never seen anything like this great monster."

"Where does it come from? What direction? Where does it go?" Crowley leaned forward in his seat, his eyes locked on Whittaker's face.

"It comes from the east, down the line we've laid out. And it runs down the line and continues on, moving the same way we're planning to lay the track." Whittaker shook his head and felt a chill run through his body. "It's a real thing, Jonathan. I've seen it. I've felt the ground move with the weight of it as it goes past. But when I look the next morning, there's no sign that it was ever here."

Crowley took a sip of his whiskey and savored it. "No sign it was ever here, just a missing person or two? Are you sure they aren't just running away? From what I saw coming into town it looks like the sort of work a person could run from."

Whittaker scowled in thought and shook his head. "The work is hard, Jonathan. I know that, but I pay a fair wage, and I don't drive them as hard a few other men I know. There're few that would run from here without gathering their pay first, anyway."

Crowley leaned back in his seat and nodded. "Never met too many who would walk away from their money without proper cause."

"I need your help, Jonathan. I'm asking."

Crowley closed his eyes and sighed. "You're asking. And here I am." He rose from his seat and reached for his coat and hat. "Does it come at any particular time? This train of yours?"

"No. It just…it only comes out at night."

"Of course. Of course it does." His voice was low and seethed with anger. Whittaker held his breath, suddenly intensely afraid of the man in his office.

He released the breath in a long, soft sigh as soon as Crowley stepped into the cold day and closed the door to his office.

---

The tiniest shavings of wood fell away from the carving in Crowley's hands as he looked at the workers earning their meager pay. He could whittle with his eyes closed. He often did, in fact. Even from a distance the men and the area stank. The men carried the stench of too many hours' labor and too little fresh water to bathe in. The camp smelled of rotting meat, hot tar, wood fires, human waste and other, less pleasant things best not considered too closely.

Crowley examined the tiny wooden train engine he'd been carving and put away his knife. The wood was durable enough on the piece and though he had been years without seeing a train, he suspected the likeness to an actual steam engine wasn't too far off.

One of the men supervising the workers let out an incoherent bellow and judging by the reactions, it was a call for the men to clean up and head on their ways. That made sense, as the sun was only a few moments from setting.

Not far away a small gathering of children who were too damned young to be out in this sort of environment stood around and looked at Crowley as if he just might be either something of great interest or something dangerous. Just possibly both.

Looking at the local children made him want to go back to a real city. Possibly just to New York, but more likely he'd be heading back to Europe soon. The New World was proving less savory than he'd hoped it might and despite his best efforts to stay away from the sort of things that fed on human suffering, here he was, waiting on a chance to hunt and kill something that should never have existed.

He was called the Hunter for a reason, but he didn't have to like it.

Two women called out from the closest brothel. They were fairly young and had managed to dress themselves in decent enough clothing. The children looked toward them and as a unit ran toward the house of ill repute. That explained why they looked relatively well fed. Some of them were likely being taken care of in hopes that when the time came, they could make good money for a living.

And that was enough of a reason for him to be in a bad mood. Not that it changed much from place to place. England, France, Italy and now here, he saw children who were far too young turned into playthings for the depraved.

One of the children looked back toward him for a moment, and on an impulse he tossed the small train toward the thin form. The child—he couldn't be sure because of the heavy coat, but he thought the face belonged on a boy—caught the train and smiled and was suddenly beautiful. Amazing how often a smile did that. He resisted the urge to smile back and instead headed for the train tracks that had already been laid, and for the distant tunnel that had been ripped into one of the hills to accommodate the very same tracks.

The rails were clean and fresh, the ground still dark from the recent work, not yet faded by sunlight and weather. The lumber was fresh and every spike that should have been driven into the ground was exactly where it should be. The work was quality, in other words.

The ground crunched under his feet, frozen moisture giving out under the weight of his tread. He stopped, closed his eyes and listened for a moment. The mass of people behind him was breaking apart. Heading toward their different destinations. Most of them were not important to him. The only exception was the sole figure he could hear heading toward him.

He opened his eyes and grinned. Now and then life was kind to him.

The voice that called out was deep and soft and spoke in Mandarin. "I know you. You hunt the demons."

He turned to the voice and saw a stout, older man looking back at him. The coolie lowered his eyes as a sign of respect. Crowley responded in the same tongue. "I have not been to China for a very long time."

"You killed my grandfather when he came back from death. He came to feed on his family, on all of us, and you stopped him." There was no question in the man's voice. Merely a statement of fact.

"I did what was asked."

"There are bad things here. Evil things."

"That's why I'm here. I've been asked to help again."

The man nodded his head and pointed toward the distant tunnel. "It comes from there. I have seen it."

"What does it do?"

The man's weathered face finally turned up toward his and the dark eyes looked into his with visible fear. "What all demons do. It eats and eats and leaves behind the screams of the dead."

"Do you know why it is here?" Crowley took a small step toward the man, careful not to spook him. The man was already unsettled. That tended to happen when people met him and found him unchanged after decades.

The man shook his head and then looked away. "I think it was called."

"Who called it?"

"Not a person. A thing. I think it was called by the blood. By the deaths."

"There are a lot of deaths here?"

"Almost every day someone dies. Sometimes they work too hard. Sometimes they are killed for their possessions." He stared at Crowley now and stepped closer. His hand reached out as if he was tempted to touch and then withdrew as if he had considered the possible consequences and decided not to take the chance. "You do not look the same, but you are the same. How is that?"

"You do not look the same as when you were a child. Yet you are the same."

He shook his head almost violently and stared harder at Crowley. "No. I mean you look like them now. You do not look like a man from the Forbidden City."

"I have been to the Forbidden City, but I am not from there."

"Your skin has changed. Your eyes have changed."

Crowley smiled and the man recoiled. "And yet I am still only me."

"Yes. I see that. Of course." The man backed away as fast as if he'd accidentally stepped on a rattlesnake's tail.

"Go on with you now. Go eat your food and I will hunt your demon."

The man spoke no more, but instead headed for the camp and the other workers walking with haste and not looking back.

Crowley watched him go as the shadows spread across the ground and merged with the gathering darkness of a starless night. He stared at the tunnel entrance in the distance, and waited as the night consumed the world around him.

Slate found him in the darkness. Crowley barely looked up. "You find out anything worth knowing?"

The man squatted next to him and stared at the tunnel. "Not much. Got a Chinaman talking about how you came here to save everyone."

"Nice to have someone thinks I'm capable." He looked toward his companion's face. "Anyone give you trouble?"

"Thing I noticed since I changed is no one ever gives me trouble anymore." He smiled and pointed his chin at the tunnel. "What's the plan?"

"I'm going to wait right here. I want to see what comes from that tunnel."

"And what do you want me to do?"

"Watch from a distance and see what there is to see. Let me know if I miss anything."

"You still trying to keep me safe?"

"Not sure if you need help with that, Slate."

"Like as not I don't." The man stood up. "Still, you keep trying."

Crowley shook his head. "Just head toward town and keep a watch for me, will you? I need to know what this thing does when it shows up."

Slate nodded and left Crowley on his own to wait for something that shouldn't have been possible.

And though it took a while, he was rewarded for his patience.

The darkness was complete and a good number of people had gone to sleep by the time the train came again. The ground started to rumble first. He could feel the vibration through the soles of his boots and the fingers of his left hand, which at that moment was resting on the cold soil.

A moment later the wind shifted and the cold air grew a touch warmer, then warmer still, until it was nearly as hot as a lover's breath. Crowley felt himself tense and forced his muscles to relax. He took in a deep breath and exhaled, and as he did the light began to show itself in the bowels of the tunnel. The tracks curved substantially enough that he could not see the far end of the tunnel, but he could see the tracks in the distance and knew that he should have seen anything the size of a train engine coming in his direction, even in the darkness.

So when the great, glaring light grew brighter he squinted his eyes against it and braced himself for something that should not exist in the world.

Something that should not be, but insisted upon coming into his view just the same.

The great black shape filled the tunnel, a solid darkness that seemed heavier than the night. The light that vomited from the tunnel was diseased. It should have caused his pupils to dilate but did not. Instead, it illuminated the world it touched with leprous awareness. The ground shook and the nocturnal creatures—and there were plenty around despite the cold weather—took flight, running from the thing coming from that pit in the side of the mountain.

The front of the engine was easily three times his height, possibly even four. The great cow pusher at the front gleamed dully in the deathly pale cast from the single burning light. There were no numbers cast in the iron front, nor painted on the metal surface, but there were shapes pressed to the metal, odd symmetries that did not sit comfortably on the eye. The sides of the engine bore great curved ribs that looked too much like they belonged to a skeletal form for Crowley's comfort. This was an engine, yes, but he doubted human hands had built it.

Was it steam that spilled from the great engine? Possibly, but Crowley had his doubts. Steam followed certain natural laws and the greasy substance spilled from the engine and flowed along the sides of the vast machine, half obscuring it from view, even as the darkness tried in vain to hide it away. The thick clouds of fog bore half-seen shapes, wretched forms that writhed and twisted as surely as hanged men at the ends of their nooses. Pistons rose and fell, wheels churned along the freshly laid tracks, and the great roaring engine pulled from the tunnel, dragging cars blacker than the night. That darkness was only broken by the windows into the interiors of the cars and each of those in turn showed sights not meant to be seen by sane men. Within those windows people suffered: they screamed silently as they faced out toward the world, and they pressed their miserable faces to the glass and searched in vain for anyone to help them escape their miseries. Some were deathly pale, others bathed in crimson stains. Some bore diseased flesh and others sported wounds that must surely have been fatal. All of them screamed. All of them wailed silently into the night, seeking a way free from their prison.

Jonathan Crowley's skin pimpled into goose flesh as he stared.

He had seen such things before, but never in this form, in this shape.

The last time Crowley'd seen so much suffering had been on a ship called from the depths by necromancers. That had gone…poorly.

He rose from his crouching position and stared at the vehicle as it slowly gathered speed, the great clouds of condensation growing thicker as the whistle on the engine let loose a scream worthy of a dozen murder victims. He looked along the tracks that the train was using and saw the lights of the town. According to Whittaker, if he didn't stop the train someone, or possibly several people, would disappear, stolen by the black train.

"Nothing for it then," he mumbled to himself. And then he started running.

The train was enormous but still gathering its speed for whatever journey it intended to make. Jonathan Crowley ran for all he was worth, as if something as vile as the vehicle itself was pursuing him, and he caught up with the great, lumbering thing before it made the first hundred feet past the tunnel. His hand caught the black surface and he felt his teeth clench. The metal was cold and felt wrong, more like mummified flesh and bone than steel. Crowley held on despite a desire to let go and fall away from the vile presence.

The texture was wrong, but the design was the same. He held onto a train, no matter that it surely wasn't made by human hands. He could see the bolts driven into metal and wood that held the thing together. He could lean forward and see the couplings between the cars. It was there he needed to go. Far easier to get to the engine from the inside, he suspected. No matter how much more dangerous the idea might be.

There were ladders to the roof of the train. There were couplings for the boxcars, but there were no doors. No possible escape for the wretches locked inside.

To the top, then.

He climbed the ladder quickly, feeling far too exposed as he clung to the side of the moving beast. His coat rippled in the wind and snapped like wings along his back, baring the Peacemakers on his hips. They were hardly worth carrying at the moment, but he carried them just the same. He might yet find a way into the train, and if he did it was hard to say what he might find.

Crowley rose to the top of the train and balanced as best he could as the beast lurched and started gathering speed. The stench of the writhing clouds escaping the engine was enough to make Coal Pit's air seem refreshing.

He moved quickly, keeping his balance as he charged toward the engine at the front of the train. There was a sense of urgency, of course, because the town was not far away now and he was supposed to stop the impossible train from taking anyone else.

He'd have thought it impossible for anything to catch his attention save the train itself, but the solitary rider off to his left, away from the town, did just that. He could make out little save horse and rider, but he was aware that the rider was watching him.

There would be time for that later, assuming he didn't get himself killed.

The open back of the engine beckoned. He saw no sign of a conductor, stoker, nor driver, but the grate to the furnace was open and he could feel the heat radiating from it; hear the screams coming from deep within the fiery bowels. Madness.

Crowley held his balance as the great train lurched again and then jumped, clearing the brief distance to the engine room's blackened floor. The heat continued. He looked at the door to the engine's furnace and kicked it shut with his heel. The metal swung easily enough and he was grateful. He could think of better ways to die than falling into a blazing fire pit.

He had never been in the engine of a train. He had no idea what it should have looked like, but surely there were supposed to be controls, something more than the deep fire burning before him.

Crowley looked around carefully, and backed away from the grate. It seemed wise, as the damned thing had opened again when he wasn't looking.

The air was too hot to breathe easily and he stepped back, unsure of what to do next. There was no one he could talk to, no one to stop, not that he could see. And that possibly meant his only recourse was to find a way back into the cars themselves.

The engine roared and great gouts of flame belched from the grate. The whistle ahead of him shrieked in outrage, and the entire train jumped forward hard enough to knock him from his feet.

Madness. This was wrong. None of what he was looking at made the least bit of sense to him.

He needed to speak to someone who knew trains, knew what he should be looking for; what, if anything, should be driving the black engine. Fear pulled at his stomach and Jonathan Crowley stood up again, grabbing at the solid wall to keep his balance.

He climbed from the engine and slipped back along the side of the train until he could climb aboard the first of the boxcars. He could feel the heat of the locomotive engine behind him and the dreadful cold of the car radiating into his hands, and through his boots, the soles of his feet.

Crowley looked around and saw that he was almost to Coal Pit. He also saw exactly what he'd hoped to see between himself and the town; Lucas Slate standing near the tracks and looking in his direction. He pointed toward the figure he'd seen earlier and Slate nodded, moving in that direction in a hurry. The man had changed in the short time they'd known each other. Crowley remained uncertain if the changes were for the better, but at the very least he seemed more capable of handling any dangers that came his way.

There was no time to think about Slate any longer. He needed to understand the train. Not knowing ate at him, tore at him, and filled him with a growing anger. It did not belong in the world and he no longer wished to tolerate that. His hands found purchase on the overhang of the roof and he peered along the side of the car, the wind catching at him threatening to tear him away from the train.

Through the window closest to him he saw the faces looking from inside, wailing silently in their miseries. They reached for him, begged him for release from their endless suffering.

He looked away. There was nothing in him for the dead.

Nothing but that damned useless sense of guilt.

Still, there was a possible access point. He held to the overhang and reached for the window and then struck the thick glass to no avail. After a second try he then reached for the Peacekeeper on his hip. The dead inside did not flinch as he took careful aim and then fired at the glass. The bullet struck and the glass spider-webbed but did not break. He fired at the same spot a second time and the rupture grew, but still the window did not shatter. Finally, a third shot and the window exploded inward.

The gun went back into its holster and Crowley looked at the ruptured opening, trying to see what might be waiting past the faces of the dead.

The dead within the boxcar reached out, possibly seeking a method of escape, but if that was their goal it seemed a miserable failure. The fearsome winds of the moving train caught at their vaporous flesh and pulled it apart, dispersing them like so much mist. Did it hurt them? Doubtful. They were already dead. Just the same they pulled back from the opening, recoiling from the tearing force of the wind. And Crowley swung himself around, grabbing at the frame of the shattered window, wincing as the shards cut at his hand and drew lines of agony along his fingers and his palm.

Coal Pit was just ahead and the train sped up, the wheels thundering along the tracks, the engine roaring and straining. He swung his body around and hooked his foot into the broken window, balancing his weight on the roof of the car and the opening into the interior.

It should have been easy enough to fight his way in past the harsh winds.

It was made easier when something grabbed his boot and pulled, dragging his leg into the boxcar. There was no time to fight and no chance to pull back, whatever had him was simply too powerful to resist. Crowley made himself go limp and let go of the overhang. The human body is not as flexible as a length or rope. His body slammed against the side of the car and his hat sailed away as he felt powerful hands grabbing, pulling, clawing at his legs until he was halfway into the car. He fought the temptation to tense up, to defend himself. Regardless of what he did at this point he was going to get tossed around, but for a moment he was powerless, and he hated that sensation.

And then he was inside, his body battered and bashed in the process. The shards of glass broke against his body and tore at him: his arms, his chest and his face, leaving scrapes and more angry red marks. The mad howling of the wind stopped as he was finally pulled inside. The rumble of the train continued but was muted.

Not that he noticed much about the sounds just then. He was too busy looking at the figures of the dead that in turn were staring at him with a hungry sort of desperation.

The dead fell upon him like a wave, reaching for him and covering him.

One face looked down at him and wept. One familiar face that he had seen very recently.

The train's whistle screamed again, a long, bleating note.

---

Whittaker paced in his small office, wondering where Crowley could have gotten himself off to. The sun was up and noon was only a short time away and still the man had not shown up. The idea that the man might have died crossed his mind but he pushed it aside quickly, unwilling to accept the possibility. He needed Crowley too much to imagine the man failing him. His entire career, his livelihood and his future with the Northern Pacific Railroad depended on the man. How could he possibly fail?

Had Crowley actually been working for him, he might well have fired the bastard.

Whittaker frowned and considered Jonathan Crowley's demeanor. No. On second thought, he'd never be quite that brave or that suicidal.

When the stranger opened his door there was no knock. Instead, the chalk-skinned man simply walked inside, ducking his head to accommodate the hat he was sporting. He wore enough leather and feathers to make Whittaker think he was dealing with an Indian for a moment, but the skin was far too pale and the features were wrong. Had he been forced to guess, he would have suspected the albino was likely born of slaves.

Before he could protest the man spoke out loud and shut away his potential objections. "Crowley sent me. He needs to talk to you. Needs to show you something a ways back on the rails."

There was no serious consideration of argument. Crowley had come to help him and so he now felt obligated. Also, Crowley still scared the sin out of him. Far better merely to do as he was told in this circumstance.

Nearly an hour later Whittaker and the stranger—a quiet, gaunt man called Slate—dismounted their horses and looked at the tunnel Whittaker's men had spent close to a month blowing through the hillside before they could even consider laying tracks. That sort of obstacle was the stuff of logistical nightmares. He hated that part of the job.

Crowley was waiting for him, his face set in hard, grim lines and his clothes dusty and worn as if he'd spent the last few years digging the damned hole in the hillside with his bare hands.

"Jonathan? What happened to you? You look...well, you look like you've been rolled in mud and kiln-dried."

"I took a ride on your ghost train." Crowley's voice was low and dry, and the anger in his words fully matched the expression on his face. "It was not a ride I much enjoyed."

Whittaker stared at him, not quite sure what to say for a moment. "You found it then? You stopped it?"

Crowley's thin mouth twitched and his brown eyes glared hard at Whittaker's face. "I found it. I rode it. I did not stop it. I'm sure if I *can* stop it."

"What? Why not?" His voice was far more demanding than he intended. Happily, it didn't seem that Crowley much cared.

"Because you and your people did something when you dug through this hill, Whittaker. You broke something that wasn't meant to be broken. I can't fix it. I don't know what it is or how to make repairs. All I know is that the result is your damned ghost train."

As he spoke the man came closer, his face locked in an expression of cold fury. "How many people have died working for you, Whittaker? How many have died working for your precious railroad?"

Whittaker stared long and hard at Crowley, carefully considering his words before he answered. "People die, Jonathan. There are accidents, and attacks by the local savages, and there are bad conditions that we have to work through. There's not much to be done about those things. They can't be helped, but every man who works for me knows the risks when he signs up."

"And where have you buried these men? Did you ship them back home?"

Whittaker shook his head and frowned. "If they made arrangements of their own, they are shipped home. If they didn't there are undertakers out here who can take care of the matter."

"Truly?" Crowley frowned. "Did you know my associate here, Slate, used to work as an undertaker? Buried half the people on Carson's Point before the town was abandoned. He knows something about burying bodies." The tone was unsettlingly conversational and didn't match Crowley's expression at all.

Whittaker turned to face Slate. The man nodded his head slightly but otherwise made no gesture to show he was even paying attention to the conversation.

Crowley continued on. "We had a little chat before I sent him to get you. According to him there isn't a single undertaker in your little town of Coal Pit. Nor could he find anyone who knew of anyone in the last month who buried a single body around here."

"What the hell does that have to do with the train?" Whittaker didn't like the way the conversation was going. He had done nothing wrong and refused to be blamed for what the local towns did or did not do to take care of matters.

"There are harbingers of the dead, spirits of the dead, conveyors of the dead. Each one is different and a lot of them come with their own cultures." Crowley shrugged as he spoke.

"What?"

"According to a lot of myths there are certain creatures, like ravens, for instance, that work to guide the dead to where they are going. Valkyries would take the spirits of warriors to their final resting places, ravens would do the same. Sometimes, they would even bring the dead back and let them have a try at revenge. Trust me, that's not a situation you ever want to deal with." He looked away. "Bastards are almost impossible to stop."

"What are you talking about, Jonathan?"

"I'm talking about you and your damned railroad, Whittaker." Crowley laughed; it was not a pleasant sound. "You've gone and created your own new Valkyrie. That damned ghost train isn't here to take the living anywhere. It's here to take the spirits of the dead to their final resting places."

"I don't understand."

"Frankly, I don't either. All I know for sure is that the train isn't taking living people away. It's taking the spirits of the dead."

"Then how did you get taken away?"

"I climbed on the damned thing myself, didn't I? Because I thought I was stopping it from taking living people away." The look Crowley shot him was a withering one, and Whitaker flinched, taking two steps back without even thinking.

"What happens now?" Oh, he hated to ask that question. He was terrified to ask it, because in his experience, when Jonathan Crowley was around the answers were almost always grim.

Crowley smiled. "Nothing."

"Nothing?"

"I don't help the dead. I never have. It's not what I do."

Not far away, Slate coughed into his hand to hide a laugh. Whittaker shot a look at the man and felt a flurry of cold fear lance through his stomach.

"But what about the train?"

Crowley shrugged. "Nothing much to do about it, Whittaker. The conductors of the dead have always been around. But there's one thing you might want to consider."

"What's that?"

Crowley looked at him, his eyes cold and level, unflinching. "I mentioned harbingers of the dead before. Banshees, black dogs, and a few other creatures that don't actually cause deaths, they just give warning cries. According to legends the only people who can hear them are the ones for whom death is coming."

"I don't understand."

"Slate over there, he did me the service of asking the people in Coal Pit about your train. Seems only three people in town heard that train in the last few days. You, an old shaman who rode out here to find the train last night and one Chinaman."

"Impossible. I heard the train myself."

"I know you did." Crowley shook his head, the smile fading away. "The old shaman, he's been watching every night for the last few evenings, knowing his time is short. A raven came and told him to wait here for his chance to meet something called the Great Spirit. I'm guessing that's his name for God. Least ways, that's what he told Slate last night. The Chinaman that heard the train died last night. He was killed just a little while after the sun set. He crossed paths with the wrong people and they cut his throat."

"I don't understand."

"Your train carries the dead away. But I think it's also a harbinger. I think it warns the people who are soon to die that death is coming for them."

Whittaker shook his head. "But I heard that train. I've heard it every night for over a week."

Crowley looked hard at him. "That's my point, Whittaker. If something unnatural were coming for you I might be able to stop it. But the only unnatural thing I've encountered here is the train."

Whittaker considered his words and shook his head.

"You have to help me, Jonathan!"

"Not much I can do here, Whittaker. No more than I could do for Robert Bragg or Loraine Haliwell. Sometimes things can't be stopped."

Crowley headed for his horse, ignoring Whittaker's pleas. A moment later Slate walked after him. Behind them Bram Whittaker fell to his knees and sobbed, seemingly lost in his miseries.

The two men climbed on their horses and started away, and while Slate stopped to look back several times, Crowley never bothered.

Almost an hour later, when they were well away from Coal Pit, Slate spoke up. "Why didn't you offer him any comfort? Why didn't you even lie about his death?"

Crowley didn't bother looking around when he answered. "Some people don't deserve comfort. Bram Whittaker isn't a decent man. I have nothing kind to offer him."

"Then why did you help him?"

"I came here because I thought people needed help, not because he was one of them."

"If only the people who will die soon can see the train, why could we see it?"

That question made Crowley actually turn and look at him. "Because neither of us is quite human anymore, Slate. Hell, I'm still not sure what you are, but I intend to find out."

Slate nodded his head in response and the two of them rode south, away from the railroad and from the things that men created by design and by accident alike.

# The Devoted

## Part One: The Town

There were things out in the hills that had no right to be there. Daniel Murdock would have bet his soul on that notion, and he was not a man who much liked the idea of losing his only chance for salvation.

He'd come west to see about saving the people heading for the promises of gold and the temptations of a wild land. To his way of thinking they needed saving more than most.

Sadly, the people he'd been traveling with did not seem to agree. To that end they'd robbed him of most his worldly possessions after he'd tried one time too many to save their souls (It did not cross his mind that his trying so desperately to save young Elizabeth's soul in the privacy of his tent would have anything to do with their behavior. Daniel Murdock was many things, but overly bright was not among them.).

That left Daniel riding on the horse he'd brought with him. He was not quite certain if that was a kindness, however, as the animal genuinely hated him. Every morning when he went to saddle the ornery beast it glared at him with murderous intent and fidgeted throughout the process of being prepped for the day. Also, the old roan liked to swat him with her tail whenever possible.

He would endure these troubles as he had so many before. He had a sacred quest and he would not falter. Salvation was his mission in life, his divine calling, and he intended to see it through. No matter how much the local scenery made him nervous. He was from New York City, and the wide-open spaces, while not completely foreign to him, often seemed too exposed. Every hill, every small dip in the landscape seemed like a place where anything at all could be lying in wait to attack.

Daniel Murdock was not a brave man, but he was determined to become one. He would do what had to be done in order to spread the gospel of his Lord and savior.

Something rustled in the bushes. Not a small sound as he had grown used to, but a loud crunching noise that involved the snapping of at least two separate thick branches.

Daniel turned to see what might be making the racket.

The shrubbery along the side of the narrow, twisted path he rode was heavy and laced with thorns. Even from a dozen feet away he could see wooden barbs thrusting in all directions. He could also see something moving in those shadowy bushes, something dark and large enough to make him wonder how it could possibly conceal itself within the confines of the greenery.

He desperately wished that his fellow travelers had been kind enough to leave him with a weapon. They had not. But they had offered him one solid piece of protection and his hands reached for the Good Book as surely as some might reach for a rifle or a pistol. The word of the Lord was a powerful tool, indeed.

His fingers wrapped tightly around the spine of his Holy Bible and he felt immediately comforted.

"Get thee behind me, foul beast." He did not merely mutter the words. He spoke them with a commanding voice.

The growl that came from the shrubs was deep, loud, and exactly enough to send the nag running. There was no warning; just the sudden bolt of the old horse's legs and without any chance to prepare himself, Daniel sailed off the horse's backside. A moment later he was on his back in the dust and trying to understand exactly how he got there. The impact was enough to knock all the wind out of him.

The damned horse did not stop running.

Daniel sat up and looked around, even as he tried to catch a breath. No luck there. His lungs didn't want to work. He managed a few shallow gasps, but not much more than that.

While he was working on finding a way to breathe, the thing in the bushes stepped out.

Daniel stopped worrying about how to catch his breath around the same time the cold hand wrapped around his ankle. By the time he'd been hauled into the thorn patch and lost a few inches of skin to the wooden skewers of the bush, he was more worried about screaming than he was about breathing.

A moment or so later, he stopped worrying about anything at all.

———

Sometimes Jonathan Crowley thought the damned rains would never stop. Other times he suspected the snow would wear him down. Then there were the places where the sun cooked a man inside his skin and left him feeling like he could never get away from the blistering heat.

Currently it was the heat. The plains were lush and green here and he could imagine that farmers of all types might one day make the most of the area, but for now most of what he surveyed was untouched by human hands. That didn't stop the damn heat though. It just meant he could get a sip of water if he felt the notion.

Really, he just didn't much like the weather. It tended to be beyond his control more often than not. There were exceptions, of course. There were always exceptions. Those were the things that made life tolerable after a few lifetimes.

The sky was clear. There was that at least. The hat on his head was enough of a shield from the worst of the heat and he was rather pleased by that notion. He liked the hat. It fit just the right way.

"You've got that look on your face again." The voice was soft, with a cultured southern drawl, and just exactly the right sort of raspy to make a man want to check if someone was dancing on his gravesite. There was a hint of humor to the voice and Crowley found that annoyed him at the moment.

"What look is that, Mister Slate?" He turned to his companion. There was nothing new to see, the same dark suit over long, thin limbs. The same top hat, a mortician's attire, which seemed fitting, as the man had been an undertaker before becoming something more than human. Slate's skin was bone pale and his features were gaunt, drawn tight over his bones. He had full lips and a broad nose, but still managed to look nearly cadaverous. His eyes were the things most people noticed even more than the stark white hair. His eyes were so pale blue as to almost seem white.

"You tend toward distraction when you're bored, Mister Crowley. By that I mean you tend to *look* for distractions. I do believe you're getting bored. I can't begin to fathom a different reason for you to study the plains so intently otherwise."

"I told you before, I intend to examine the flora and fauna of this continent to my satisfaction."

Slate's smile bordered on insulting. "Yes, but the grass is the same as it was before and so are the birds."

"I've no intention of starting grief, Mister Slate."

Slate waved one hand as if batting away a fly. "You never do. I have long since come to accept that grief will find you just the same." To prove his point Slate nodded toward the path ahead of them. Just at the horizon a solitary figure stood waiting, unmoving in the blistering heat. "Perhaps the gent up there will help accommodate your desires." Even as he spoke Slate checked his pistols. They were easily reached, as was the rifle he had tucked next to his saddle. The man was fair enough with his handguns, but as Crowley—and over a dozen unfortunate fools—had already learned, he was an absolute terror at long ranges.

Crowley stared at the raggedy figure up ahead. There was a very slight breeze and it shifted the clothing on the dark shape they approached.

"Now what do you make of that?" Crowley was barely aware that he was speaking. He leaned a bit forward in his saddle and tapped his heels against the stallion's sides. The horse responded by increasing his pace. A moment later, as the winds picked up, Slate was following suit.

They rode up to the raggedy shape that stood, but seemed to dance just the same. The harsh winds caught the fabric and snapped the edges.

Crowley's eyes looked the form over carefully, as if he had found a new and different form of plant life. The rest of his long face remained expressionless, however. Slate stared as well, but his features showed his disgust.

Someone had taken the time to kill several different animals and then very carefully assemble the bones of those animals into a new shape. Femur bones, rib cages, the tiny digits of rabbit paws and coyote and possibly even a wolf, all worked together into a larger form that mocked the human shape. The entire affair had been pasted together with mud and either left to dry or possible even baked until it was finished. There were enough scorch marks on the bones to make him think the latter.

"What would make a person do such a thing?" Slate's voice was as raspy as ever as he shook his head.

Crowley lifted a part of the cloak with careful fingers, holding the edge of the ratty material as if it might try to take a bite out of him, and examined the back of the shape. It was more of the same, bones and rot and mud all cooked together into a rough form.

"There's no writing on it. That's something, I suppose."

"What would writing matter?"

"Words have power, Mister Slate. The right words in the right order can cause some truly spectacular disasters."

Slate looked at his companion for a moment with a worried expression. "Is there power in this thing?"

Crowley shook his head. "On that subject this thing reminds me of you. There's something. I'm not sure yet just what that something might be."

Crowley looked past the totem and then pointed down the path a ways where buildings had been slapped together with a good deal of haste and an appalling lack of skill. "I suppose if we were so inclined we could head there to find out more about what is happening here."

Slate's hand once again rested on the butt of his revolver. Later, when he was alone and thinking, he would contemplate exactly when he'd started seeking comfort in cold steel and polished wood grips. "And are we planning on heading into that town this day, Mister Crowley?"

Crowley looked down the road and contemplated the buildings. The winds calmed a bit and he let go of the flapping cloth wrapped around the totem. "I have a mind to head in that direction. Should I feel a need to stop there, I might. But it is not yet in my plans."

Slate let out a very deliberately dramatic sigh. "Well then, I suppose we should see what we shall see."

"It could be nothing at all, Mister Slate."

"I have learned that there is seldom 'nothing at all' in situations which involve your person, Mister Crowley." His voice was as dry as the baked mud of the totem's uneven surface.

Crowley smiled. Most people would have flinched a bit, but Slate had seen that smile plenty of times and while it was still a frightening thing, he had grown moderately accustomed to it.

Crowley nudged his horse and the animal obeyed, moving toward the distant town.

Despite his common sense telling him it would be a bad idea, Slate followed. There were still things that he needed to know about himself and so far his best hope of discovery lay with the man he had seen destroy an entire town and slaughter a legion worth of Hell's minions.

---

Did the town have a name? Not as such. Still, the people who lived there called it home.

There was a river. Most times if people were going to settle, they had the common sense to have a source of water. Those that didn't seldom stayed for long.

The people who lived there all had their own stories to tell. Most of which revolved around a hope for something better in a new place. Some of them had found that something better, some had not. And isn't that always the case?

The first folks to settle in the area had built a fine-looking home. It was almost exactly at the center of the town. Two stories tall and built with a great deal of skill. Walter Perry, the man who assembled the structure with his own hands (and those of his wife and two sons, to be fair) was now the mayor of the town as much as anyone could be said to be the mayor of a place that had never once considered an election. Most times if people had questions, they came to him and asked them. And Perry, with his usual slow consideration, gave them answers. He would mull over their words as if considering the weight of each syllable, and then he would smack his lips or possibly, if the situation seemed to merit the action, actually chew on the edges of his great mutton-chopped mustache, and then speak slowly in response. Most people considered his words as carefully as he offered them and found his words carried wisdom.

Had anyone asked him if he were wise, he would surely have said not, which to many people was a sign of his wisdom. It is often a contrary world we exist in.

Just the same, when someone came along and said "Good morning, Mister Mayor," Perry would inevitably say good morning in response. To do otherwise simply seemed rude to him. Elizabeth Perry, his wife, was a wisp of a woman, not because she went hungry, but simply because that was how the Lord had made her. She was also as cheerful as her husband was stoic. She had a wonderful man who took care of her—and whom, she in turn took care of—and she had two beautiful boys, tall and strapping, that she had raised to adulthood. They were both the center of attention at many of the local functions, and most of the unwed young ladies (as well as an inappropriate number of the married ones) tended to look their way with affection and dreams of a life together. So far her boys were blissfully unaware of that fact, but she knew they would change their tunes when the time came.

Her boys, Dirk and Robert, were well mannered and well thought of. They would inherit all that she and her husband had created, including the small town they all called home.

At least that was the plan until the Preacher showed himself.

Since then the town had changed. Exactly how she was not sure she could surmise. Elizabeth Perry did not feel at home in her town any longer. People still smiled and nodded and spoke to her as they always had, but something was wrong on a fundamental level. Something had changed. The feeling was rather like looking at a sunny day and having a feeling a storm intended to blow through within a short time. A violent storm, one likely to cause grievous damage.

"Storm's coming." The words were out of her mouth and spoken aloud and she flinched at that notion. Once said, words were a hard thing to take back.

To the east she saw two men riding slowly into town along the solitary road that cut through the area. To the west she saw only the road and the fields and trees. Still her eyes were drawn to the west and her lips muttered their words again, a faint whisper, a sigh.

Elizabeth shivered in the stifling summer heat.

Something bad. That was all she needed to know. Something bad. A storm of epic scale.

The mercantile she ran with her husband did good business, but the heat of the day was keeping most people inside, it seemed. That, and there were those out in the fields, tending to their farms or their herds. The town wasn't all that large, but the farms around it added to the size.

So, she had nothing much to do but watch as the riders headed into the town proper. She made herself breathe. That seemed a challenge at the moment. She had to remind herself. That hadn't happened to her since the day she found out her parents were dead, killed in a fire at the mill her father owned. Then it was grief that made breathing a chore. Now? She wasn't quite sure. Something was bothering her. That was all she needed to know at the moment.

The riders slowed at the intersection. It wasn't much of a crossroad, but it was there. East and west cut through town. North led to the river and the newly built church. South led to the saloon and the cluster of buildings that made up the true center of commerce for the area. The mill, the blacksmith's shop and livery. The mill was run by her sons. The blacksmiths was handled by Arne Holdt, a very burly man who always managed a smile whether or not a soul had business to offer him, and the livery was situated on the back of the mercantile, where her husband could attend to the occasional business. While the Perry family was not rich by most standards, they were most certainly one of the wealthiest in the area.

All the money and security meant nothing, however, as she watched the riders coming closer.

The taller of them was unsettling. He was pale and cadaverous, with a mouth set in a half-smile, as if he were privy to a joke he had no intention of sharing. His eyes were cold in color and his clothes were black and lightly dusted with the colors of the trail. A crop of feathers had been tucked into the band of his top hat. They bobbed slowly up and down with the movements of the rider and the horse.

As uncomfortable as the first man made her, the second was worse. He looked as plain as the day is long, with brown hair, brown eyes and a longish face, but even from a distance he seethed. There was rage in that man, barely contained within his body. His expression was calm enough and his posture seemed relaxed, but it was deception. She could almost feel the rage that washed from him. Her mother had always claimed Elizabeth was "a touch Fey." Perhaps there was some truth to that. Whatever the case, the man chilled her as easily as the idea of the coming storm.

The riders stopped in front of the mercantile and the taller of the two, the pale one, looked to her and tipped his feathered top hat. "Ma'am." His voice did nothing to help calm her frayed nerves. "I wondered if you might be able to direct us to a boarding house."

Elizabeth swallowed hard and heard a clicking noise in her throat. Parched. Couldn't seem to get a decent breath and now her mouth was dry as the air of late. She pointed one hand toward the sign above her. Perry's Mercantile was in large letters, but beneath that in finer script were the words "rooms available."

The taller man nodded his head and slid from his horse with a liquid grace that should have been impossible for so gangly a shape. A moment later the other man was down as well, his brown eyes looking over her with a scrutiny she'd seldom encountered since she was a single woman and a few decades younger. Despite herself, she blushed.

"Two rooms, if you could, ma'am." The taller one spoke again. The other was looking around the town, his face as calm as the sky above and just as deceptive to her way of thinking.

They signed for the rooms after paying cash upfront. The names were Lucas Slate and Jonathan Crowley.

---

Crowley found the river with ease. He and Slate walked from the town proper and followed the path to the sound of rushing water. The waters were cool and clear and tasted sweet after too long on the road, and when they were done drinking they went their separate ways to bathe and wash away the grit of the long road trip. Simply put, they both stank of the long ride and they knew it. Fresh water, fresh attire and when they were done and their soiled clothes were packed away, both of them felt more like fit company.

The riverside was an interesting place for entirely different reasons.

Crowley bathed and took his time, savoring the feel of the cold waters washing away the road traveled and the heat of the day. He was also not quite alone as he quickly discovered. When he was finished scrubbing himself clean, he heard voices nearby and swam over to investigate. Four children sat in the shallows near a large building and washed themselves, singing hymns softly. They sang together with voices low and sweet.

Crowley paid their naked forms little heed. He was far more interested in the words coming from their mouths. They sang in words he had never heard before, in a language unknown to him.

That was rare enough to catch his attention.

He listened to the words, to the soft sweet voices that wove together into something else, something stronger even than the voices of the innocent.

He listened as they sang magic into the air, into the water and into the soil.

He did not speak.

The time for words would come later.

A distance from him, on the other side of the dark structure at the river's edge, Lucas Slate bathed and remembered the past. He recalled the times when he wouldn't have dared show his body in public for fear of being tormented. He reflected on how much his life had changed since he'd moved himself from his home in Georgia and taken himself as far west as Colorado.

His life hadn't changed. Not really. He had. He had become something so very different.

When he was done bathing his body, he lowered into the waters until he was completely submerged and he held his breath, opening his eyes to see through the slowly drifting waters. The currents carried their usual treasures, leaves and sticks and sediment. Fish swam by and a thin water snake undulated past, uninterested in him and his pale white flesh.

Fifteen minutes after he lowered himself into the water, he let himself rise back up. He exhaled the single breath he'd held for that time and slowly drew in another.

Oh, yes, he had changed. He was still changing. He knew that. He could tell it simply by looking around himself and letting his eyes go soft. That was what his father had called it. "Soft eyes," when you didn't focus on anything, you simply let your attention spread out as thin as it could and saw everything at once and nothing at all. He let his eyes go soft and saw the differences in the world around him. Not far away the trees gave off their own faint shimmer of color. The water danced with reflections of energies beyond merely the sun. The water danced with *life*. The trees held a thousand secrets and the river just as many and, just beyond the trees, the building he looked at appeared quite different when seen with soft eyes. Instead of a solid structure of boards and white wash with new glass windows and shutters, he saw a network of black vines that imitated a building and slowly dug dark roots into the soil, seeking deeper and deeper, drawing strength from the ground and spreading more dark tendrils in a slowly widening net.

There was a reason Jonathan wanted them to bathe separately. It had nothing to do with modesty and nothing to do with privacy. It had to do with perspective. He wanted to know what Slate saw, and Slate knew that.

Lucas Slate was changing. He understood that. So did Crowley. Neither of them knew exactly what Slate was becoming, but Crowley intended to find out and Slate intended to let him. How else would he ever know what he was supposed to be?

Slate slipped out of the water and dried himself with a thick cloth. A moment later he was dressing in clothes identical to those he'd already removed. The weather was simply too hot for much other than the thin attire he'd chosen earlier. The pants and shirt were first. Then the belt and his weapons and finally then the vest and jacket. As he was slipping the jacket over his torso, he became aware of the person watching him. He looked toward the wooden structure and *felt* the person watching but did not see. He should have seen. He knew that. Remarkably little escaped his notice these days. When he looked back on his past, he often felt that he'd spent most of his life blind and had only recently become aware of all that he'd missed. It might well have made some men feel betrayed, but as he was still not sure what was happening to his body and his mind—there were differences in his mind, there was no use in denying it, not even to himself—he remained uncertain as to whether or not he had received a blessing or a curse. Slate was exactly wise enough to reserve judgment for now.

Someone was watching him. Some *thing* was watching him. He slipped on his boots and did his best to ignore the creeping sensation of eyes locked on him. Too many times over the years he had felt eyes focused on him with ill intent. This felt similar. Not quite the same, not quite as malevolent, but close, so very close.

Slate doffed his hat and looked away from the building.

He climbed the gentle slope from the river and headed for the path back to town. He did not go far, merely as far as the front of the whitewashed structure. It was a simple, two-story affair, well-built and on a solid foundation.

Malevolence crept around the edges of the building, seeped through the wood.

He waited with a calm expression, one hand on the butt of his Colt Paterson. He stood that way until Crowley came walking up from the other side of the building.

Crowley nodded and never said a word. The two of them walked back toward town, not hurrying in the least and despite the temptation on his part, Slate did not look back the way they had come.

"Something was watching me."

Crowley nodded in response. He remained quiet for several yards before he spoke. "What did you make of the building?"

"I think it's a vile piece of filth, cleaned up and made pretty," Slate replied, his voice low and conversational.

Crowley nodded again, his eyes looking toward the town as they approached. "I heard children singing songs and casting sorceries like they were playing with a deck of cards." Crowley's voice was soft, and calm, and deceptive.

"What sort of magic were they casting?"

"The sort that could cause no end of trouble for the people around here."

"What will you do about it, Mister Crowley?"

Crowley smiled, just a bit, enough to make Slate flinch. "Well now, I reckon that depends on what the folks around here ask me to do about it."

"That again?"

"We all have rules we have to follow, Mister Slate. That is one of mine. I am asked to help or I do not help."

"And if I asked you to help?"

"You are not currently in a situation where you need my assistance." Crowley shrugged. Unlike Slate, he did not carry a holster or any weapons aside from a rather impressive knife strapped to one leg.

"If I should become entangled into the affairs of this town and then ask for your help?"

"Well now, that is the sort of situation where I might be obliged to lend a helping hand." Crowley nodded to a gathering of men staring at the two of them. To be fair, most of the men were goggling Slate and he knew it. He had always struck people's attention, a side effect of being an albino. These days with the changes going through his body, he stood out even more, and most folks tended to watch him as if he were a dancing bear: amusing and potentially dangerous. According to Crowley he wasn't really all that amusing. That left potentially dangerous. He was decidedly that. Even he wasn't sure exactly how dangerous he might be. Another mystery in a long line of unsolved riddles.

They moved back to town. The sun would be setting soon and they were tired, the both of them.

———

The children gathered together on the porch in front of the white building and, after conferring, decided it was time to tell the preacher what they had seen. They did not knock. The white structure was a church, and no one needed to ask permission to enter the house of the Lord, that was what the preacher told them.

Lorraine was the oldest, all of ten, and so it fell to her to wake the man from his slumbers. She walked up to his private room and knocked on the door four times before she entered the room and moved to his bed.

The man lay in darkness, as he often did when the sun was at its brightest. He claimed the heat of the day got to him and they believed him as they believed him in all things. He was the preacher, after all, and not known for telling lies.

"Preacher?" She touched his arm and recoiled quickly. Much as Lorraine loved the preacher, his skin was cold and felt hard as stone.

He did not sit up, but he spoke to her. "What is it, child? What bothers your soul this day?"

"There are strangers in town, preacher. They came right past the guardian and walked from town over to here, to bathe in the river."

The preacher nodded his head. "I suppose I should meet the newcomers?"

Lorraine, who often helped by being the eyes of the preacher when he was resting, nodded her head in response. "Josiah said that one of them, a tall, pale man, saw the house with eyes that see too much."

"That could well be a problem, my child. Thank you for that."

The preacher sat up and moved his hands over the rawness where his face should have been. "Lorraine, my child? Would you be a dear and get my mask for me?"

"Yes, sir." She smiled and reached for the heavy wooden box. When the mask was in her hands she cringed a bit at the feel of the materials. It was uncomfortable to feel the way the fabric and leather moved across her fingertips. Still, she felt honored to slip the mask over his head and watched with awe as the materials worked themselves into his skull and fused with him.

The preacher was a great man.

He stood up and rolled his shoulders, which creaked and groaned like the boards on a ship. She knew that because she'd come from England with her family only a few years earlier. Her family was gone now, of course, but the preacher was here and took care of her and the other children.

And they, in turn, took care of him.

He held out one hand and Lorraine took it, feeling the hard surface of his skin through the thin gloves. "Come child. Show me to the strangers."

"Of course, preacher." She smiled up at him and he looked down, his eyes dark within the mask but she knew him well enough to know that somewhere within the confines of that structure he was smiling back.

"What will you do to them, preacher?" she asked as they walked down the stairs. The sun was just setting and heat of the day was already abating.

"Well now, I suppose first I shall meet them and we shall see if they know the word of our Lord and Savior."

"Amen," she replied and it was good.

It was always good in the presence of the preacher.

## Part Two: The Rabble

"You know we are being followed, Mister Crowley?" Slate's voice was as soft and sepulchral as ever.

"By two children." Crowley nodded his head.

"Do you plan to do anything about them?"

"I most certainly do not." Crowley's lips pursed into a flash of a smile. "Currently they are doing a lovely job of keeping me amused."

"Amused?"

"They are as subtle as a pack of drunken miners celebrating a proper gold strike, Mister Slate. Every move they make is comical simply because they do not realize how loud they are."

"You have an odd sense of humor, you know that?"

"Stick around a few hundred years and you'll be amazed by the things that can make you laugh."

As Slate had no response to that, he let it go.

They finished their slow amble back into town, both of them clean and wearing fresh clothes. When they entered the Perry Mercantile the same woman was still there, looking at them with wide eyes and a dubious expression. Slate found it a bit amusing that she spared more nervous glances toward Crowley than toward him, despite the fact that he was the one speaking with her. After a few simple exchanges he'd negotiated the cost of having their road-stained clothes washed and delivered.

After that he looked to Crowley. He merely smiled as he headed from the building and back into the light of the day.

Said light was fading as the sun slid toward the west. Not long before the night came to take over again. It had been a surprisingly eventful day after a few weeks of riding horses with little but the occasional rabbit or deer for company...and dinner. The totem outside the unnamed ramshackle town, the odd building that was either growing from the ground or digging its way into the soil near the river, and of course the two children who were following them and failing at being discreet.

Slate looked to his companion, "Where did you plan on heading now?"

"I am feeling the need for a drink. There's a saloon just on the other side of this building and I intend to relax a bit." Lies, all of it, but Slate knew Crowley liked his lies and tended to stick with them. He very likely had every intention of tending to the local saloon, but not with any desire to have a whiskey.

Because he felt the need to watch over the man's back, Slate followed him.

The saloon had no name and did not advertise itself, save for a small sign that said "Spirits." What it did have was a small set of tables on a wooden deck outside of the actual building and four walls that were put together to last for a while, which seemed to be the exception and not the rule in the town. Two sturdy wooden stairs led up to the porch and from there access to the actual bar was merely a matter of opening a door.

Crowley walked in first and actually slowed as he entered. Slate could see why immediately. It wasn't much of a town by most standards, but the saloon was full. True it wasn't large but every seat was taken.

And as Crowley entered the room every head turned toward the door and looked him over. He kept walking, his eyes aimed toward the wooden bar at the end of the room, and the man standing behind it and staring at him with mild surprise.

Slate walked into the room and most everyone seemed to forget about Crowley.

He was a sight to see and he knew it. Skin as white as aspen bark, hair even whiter, and a face that belonged on a cadaver. He was as tall as he was pale and he still liked dressing himself in his mortician attire. He tended to stand out. The difference was that these days, as opposed to before the change took place in him, most folks decided it was safer not to cross his path.

Having come close to wearing a noose on a few occasions, he was just fine with people being a bit more cautious.

Crowley slid up to the bar and ordered two beers. The man running the place nodded his head and then forgot all about the order as he stared at Slate. Slate stared back and narrowed his eyes until the man remembered he was supposed to be doing something.

The atmosphere in the place was tense, and Slate resisted the temptation to turn back around and leave. He was not much for confrontation. He never had been. Instead, he walked over to Crowley and gestured with his chin. "Not many places to sit down here."

Crowley's eyes scanned the place over. "I imagine we can stand for a few minutes."

A man not two feet away mumbled, "Or you could just leave."

Crowley looked his way and smiled.

"Well, damn," said Slate.

"We could," Crowley agreed. "But then we might get into a dark mood. Mister Slate is a bad man to put into a foul disposition."

Slate resisted the urge to tell Crowley not to use him as an example. Instead, he leaned over the sitting man with the rude mouth. The fellow was doing his absolute best not to be noticed. He was failing.

"I didn't mean—"

"But you did," Crowley countered. "You most certainly did. You just didn't expect us to hear you. I always say if you have something to talk about, you should speak clearly. For instance, if I were to say you were a rude, uncivilized and quite frankly unbathed swine of a man, I would make certain to say it loud enough for you to hear it." The grin was still on his face. The man stared hard at him now, working out whether or not Crowley had insulted him if the look on his face was any indication. Soon enough he realized that the stranger in town had, in fact, been less-than-complimentary.

Slate stood back. He had no particular desire to be in a fistfight. He'd never been very good with using his hands for violent reasons.

"Mister, I don't much like your tone."

"My tone is without flaw. Your manners are a very different situation."

Once again there was a pause and then the man stood up, a scowl on his face, and glared hard at Crowley. "You need to learn some manners."

Jonathan Crowley stared at the man for a long moment and the man stared back at first and then began to wither, his anger fading into dust and his resolve going away with it. Most times that might have been enough, but Crowley jammed two fingers into the man's stomach hard enough to push him backward. "You'll be wanting to leave now. Before I lose my temper."

"That's enough!" The man behind the bar was holding a shotgun. He was wise enough to aim it at the ceiling, but he was looking at Crowley and the mumbler. "I'm not much for cleaning up blood from the floors. This is a nice place and I'll keep it that way. So you feel like having any arguments, take 'em outside."

Crowley looked at the man and smiled. His hand reached into the pocket of his vest and found a few small coins, which he counted out. A moment later the coins needed to pay for two beers were on the counter. "We'll take these outside to drink then, if it's just the same." His eyes flickered to the man standing in front of him. "Something in here stinks to hell anyway."

The mumbler did not respond. Crowley walked out without bothering to look back, a mug of beer in each hand. Slate followed, doing his best not to look around nervously.

When they had settled outside at one of the small tables, Crowley took a sip of his beer and smacked his lips together noisily.

"Just feeling the need to make friends, are you?"

The other man looked at him and shrugged. "You can't see what's under the sediment in a pond if you don't stir the waters."

Slate took a deep drink of his beer and set the mug down, looking toward the door of the saloon. "I find I can often discover a few truths without offending the entire town."

"I might be able to follow that philosophy if I intended to settle down here, but as this a brief stopping point, no. I prefer to get things taken care of and then leave."

"Hadn't you claimed this was merely a place to rest?" Slate eyed his companion skeptically.

"And am I now supposed to believe you fell for that line, Mister Slate?"

"Fair enough." He found himself chuckling. To be fair the odds of staying in any town with Crowley and not running across troubles seemed slim at the best of times. After long stretches of riding or walking or simply existing, he found himself slowly coming around to the idea of liking when things happened.

There was a time when that notion would have had him running for the safety of a solid door he could lock, but he had changed. He was changing.

"There they are." Crowley spoke without moving his head, but his finger tapped the edge of his mug and then pointed. Not that far away the two young ones were watching them, one boy, one girl, both not yet at the age where they should have been far from their parents, but that had never surprised Slate very much. He had buried his fair share of children who should have been better watched over and he had warned more than a few parents about the dangers in his time.

"Do you intend to confront them then?" Slate's voice held a teasing note. "Or are they perhaps young enough to avoid offending you?"

"Most children are curious. But these two are not idle about it. They're here for a reason."

"You suppose someone sent them to watch us?"

"Mister Slate, were I a gambling man I'd wager on it."

"So now you intend to wait?"

"Exactly so, my good man."

The preacher walked slowly up the street, his head down and the flat brimmed hat placed firmly upon the top of his head. The sun was starting to set and the shadows were drawing out before him as he moved toward town.

You choose the right time of day and you can see most of the people in a town without much difficulty. The houses that had been slapped together without much consideration for the elements leaned and swayed where they usually did, though the one built by Liam Patterson had collapsed and currently the man was sorting through the pieces of his world and trying to decide how to put them back together.

The preacher came to him and placed a hand on his shoulder. Patterson's flesh was tense and bordered on feverish. "You'll stay with us tonight, Liam, if that is your will. There is room. And tomorrow we shall help you build again."

Liam's blue eyes were moist with unshed tears of gratitude. A man at the very end of his strength is often grateful for the smallest gestures. "Thank you, preacher." He lowered his head and cast his eyes upon the dirt. He was not a man who regularly attended the sermons offered by the preacher.

"We are all together in the world, Liam. We have all been helped in times of need." He did not say that the man should feel free of his guilt for not attending the sermons. He did not need to. "Find your belongings and head to the house. Tell Annie I invited you."

"I will, and thank you so much, preacher."

Without another word the preacher moved on, heading through the collection of small huts and structures still being assembled. There were many in the area that needed help and in time he would offer what he could. That was the will of the Lord.

And as he walked, and took note of the people around him, he considered the strangers his children had spoken of. Lorraine seemed worried about them. Lorraine was always worried. She was a joyous girl who felt certain that her joy would be stolen away from her without warning. The preacher intended to make sure that did not happen to her or any of his children. They had proven their devotion already, and he would not let their faith go unrewarded. He had been given his second chance at life for a reason, and he was not a man who intended to squander a second chance.

Alvin Keats looked his way and then glanced toward the closest building when he recognized the preacher.

Having been noticed it was now too late for Keats. The preacher walked his way as calmly as he walked anywhere, and the last embers of the sun's light faded behind him as he reached Keats.

"We had a discussion not long ago, Alvin, regarding the condition of your soul. Do you remember that talk?"

Keats trembled and nodded his head as he stared past the preacher. He flinched as the sun faded away.

"What was said to me regarding this very night, Alvin? Do you remember?"

"I said that I would come to you and ask salvation, preacher. I know that I said that to you. I know I did."

"Indeed you did." He nodded. The man had tried to attack him. Keats had been hungry and desperate and felt the need to steal from a man of the cloth in order to sate his needs. Being a man of God, he'd offered the would-be thief one chance at redemption.

"I meant to show myself, preacher. I meant to, but I'm weak."

The tone of his voice was off. He did not sound contrite. Keats reached to the small of his back and pulled a long-bladed knife from the sheath he hid there. "I'm a weak man, preacher, and I'm desperate. I can't worry about salvation when I have mouths to feed."

The preacher sighed and shook his head slowly, his eyes on Keats. His gaze did not waver and Keats stared back, the blade forgotten as he saw into the man's soul.

"I was transformed by the Lord, Alvin Keats. I was not a wicked man, but I was foolish. The Lord gave me one last chance to save myself, one last chance to help my fellow man, and I will not fail Him." The Preacher reached out and his hand covered Alvin Keat's fingers where they held the hilt of the Bowie knife. "The Lord said unto me that mercy was a requirement and I believed Him. He also said unto me that fools refuse mercy at their own risk."

Keats's mouth stretched into a silent scream as the blade in his hand melted. There was no warning, no glow of fire or flash of light. One second the knife was as it should be and the next molten metal drooled down over his hand and blistered the skin, cooked meat and bone alike.

He tried to fall back, but the preacher held his gaze and refused him the right to move his body.

"Consider the state of your soul, my son. Know that the next time I see you, you shall either be at my doorstep and asking for the Lord's Grace, or you shall know the agonies in your hand throughout your body and soul alike."

The preacher stepped past Keats and the man fell to his knees and screamed hoarsely. There was nothing more to say to him. The man would either come seeking salvation or he would join with the guardian the preacher had set before the town.

There was much to do and he had tasks to see to, and so the preacher left Keats to make his own decisions and headed for the children. He would know what they had.

---

Crowley looked at the children and shook his head. They were hardly what he expected. Children of that age could find something fascinating for only a few moments unless that something told them tales or held an element of risk. That was his belief and he had no reason to change it.

So, the children who'd spent the last hour watching him were a mystery.

Then again, so was the man sitting across from him. When he'd first met Lucas Slate the undertaker had been smaller, almost dainty. He had also still been human. Now he was something else and continuing to change.

"Anything interesting going on in there, Mister Slate?" He nodded his head toward the saloon.

"Currently a man named Hinders is ranting on about how he almost shot your eyes out. He's been doing that since we left the room. Otherwise, the conversation seems to be about the new local clergy. Seems he's not exactly popular with everyone, but he's gaining a flock just the same."

Jonathan Crowley eyed the children skeptically. They were still watching him like he might be the most fascinating thing they'd ever seen. They were giving Slate the same scrutiny, to be fair, but Slate looked odd enough that the reaction was fairly normal.

Slate looked toward him with a half-smile on his long face. "The children are just annoying you now, aren't they?"

"Doesn't seem right, children sitting there for so long."

Almost as if they'd heard his words, the children suddenly stood. As one they turned toward the direction they'd come from, where the last ember of the sun had faded already and the twilight was losing a battle with darkness.

And from that direction came a solitary figure. He was a very large man, larger even than Slate, and he wore a black suit and a flat-brimmed hat that hid his face in shadows.

Crowley looked at the man long enough that Slate turned in his seat to look as well.

Slate's voice was very soft, barely above a whisper. "That is not a man, Mister Crowley."

"No?" he stared closer at the figure and saw the long necklace of beads swaying with the man's steps. At the bottom of that strand was an oversized crucifix that seemed carved from bone. "Then what do you suppose he is?"

The children ran to the stranger and they both watched as the children each captured a hand in their fingers and held on to the looming stranger.

The man squatted and the little girl leaned in close and whispered in his ear.

And as she told her secrets, the man with the flat-brimmed hat slowly turned his head to look toward Crowley and Slate.

"I reckon he's about to be a problem, Mister Crowley."

Crowley slowly nodded his head. There was a feeling coming from the man that had nothing to do with crosses or children. There was a sense of menace that was almost strong enough to touch.

And as the stranger eyed the two of them that sensation or menace grew stronger.

Slate shook his head. "We should sit this out, I think, Mister Crowley."

"Sit what out?"

In answer to his question the door to the saloon slammed open and from within its depths they came, the men he'd seen earlier packed tightly into the place, all of them looking past the table where he and Slate sat, and bristling as they caught sight of the man and the children.

"Preacher!" The bartender was the one who roared the words. "You aren't welcome in this town anymore. You hear me?" The man was holding his shotgun and he looked like he was prepared to use it.

Behind and around him several other men were sorting out firearms and handguns, most of them just intoxicated enough to make the task dangerous and foolish.

Crowley felt the grin pulling at his lips and made it go away.

This was about to get interesting.

# Part Three: Crossfire

Jonathan Crowley was grinning like a fool for all of two seconds and then he suppressed it, but there was no denying he was excited. Slate took one look at his companion's face and knew it. They rode all over the countryside looking for trouble, because that was what Crowley did. He denied it constantly, often talked of how much he wished he could settle himself down and relax, and there was every reason to believe that he meant it, but with the preacher on one side of them and a gathering of angry townsfolk on the other, the man wasn't panicked in the least. He was just sitting at the table of a no-name tavern and looking at the clergyman and the children with him and waiting as calm as could be.

Lucas Slate did not feel anywhere near as calm, but he did his best to hide his worry. Long years had taught him that fear was like a flame in the darkness: people tended to notice it and be drawn to it more often than not.

"We told you, you ain't welcome in this town anymore, preacher!" The bartender was screaming the words, as if anyone around them couldn't hear him. The crowd of people with him, mostly drunk and armed with pistols, rumbled their agreement. "You need to get out of here, now."

The man he was speaking to was big, with a dark suit, a dark hat with a flat brim, and a crucifix around his neck that was the color of sun-bleached bone. The sun had set and there was little to be seen of the man beyond that, save for the little boy on one of his hands and the little girl on the other. The children had followed Slate and Crowley from the river when they'd bathed the dirt of the road off of their bodies.

Slate knew that the man was not human. He also knew that the house the man and the children dwelled in was not a house in the truest sense.

He felt the malignance of that building, and he suspected the same darkness wrapped itself around the preacher, but he couldn't concentrate well enough to know for certain. He was still new to being...whatever it was he was becoming, and he didn't know how to just make his eyes see more than they normally did, not unless he was relaxed.

There was nothing at all relaxing about their current situation. Not to Slate. Crowley seemed just fine with it though. The man was leaned back and relaxing, his eyes looking at the preacher and the children, his hands resting on the table in front of him, one finger just touching the handle of the mug holding his beer.

Slate looked away from Crowley and focused on the bartender. The man was making all kinds of noise about how the preacher should go on back to his house and leave town. "You need to take your children and leave here, preacher! We can't have you or them around decent folk, you hear me?"

The preacher had been squatting when the man came out of his bar and started screaming, but he was standing now and his hands gently urged the children behind his legs and the heavy coat he wore in the cooling evening air.

The preacher's voice was calm and soft and made Slate think of an autumn night and a cold wind coming from the north. "You've stated your case, David Parrin. I have stated mine. This is our home now, and we're not leaving. You are not the law, and I'll not have you and your fellow sinners telling me where to go when there are souls that need saving."

"Just who the hell are you calling a sinner?" The bartender took three steps toward the preacher. Like Crowley, Slate and all of the men with him, he was standing on a small porch in front of his bar. Two steps down would take him to the street. Fifteen paces from there he would be close enough to touch the preacher's hat.

He didn't have to get much closer. He was carrying a loaded shotgun.

Slate felt himself standing up, but it seemed like he was watching someone else. Surely he wasn't foolish enough to get between a man with a shotgun and the target of that man's anger. He was not a brave man. He had, in fact, always been a bit of a coward. It was a side effect of being an albino. Best to avoid getting noticed.

So it had to be someone else he heard speaking, though the voice was his and his lips were the ones flapping away. "Gentlemen, whatever your differences, you'd do well to remember there are children present." Indeed, that was his voice.

He looked to the bartender. The man was staring murder at the preacher and barely seemed to him ant mind.

The crowd near the bartender noticed him. In particular, a man named Hinders who'd nearly gotten himself into a scrap with Jonathan Crowley spoke up, made brave by the men around him and the revolver he was holding. "You should stay out of this you freak of nature. It doesn't concern you."

The words made perfect sense. Six months earlier he'd have listened. Lucas Slate would have done everything in his power to stay well away from the confrontation, because six months earlier he had not begun changing into something other than human. He had still been a man, and he had still been keenly aware of how delicate his life was.

Slate turned and pinned the man with his stare. "You need to watch that tongue of yours, boy, before I cut it out of your mouth." His southern drawl was heavier now, as if his rising ire had stirred it up.

Hinders stared at him, his flabby face showing his surprise. He was not a man who expected to be confronted often, apparently, and certainly not when he was carrying a loaded weapon.

To show how much he thought of the notion, Hinders raised the long barrel of his Walker Colt and pointed it at Slate.

And the rage took over.

In his past Lucas Slate had been burned out of his home on Savannah, Georgia, had been forced to relocate himself into the Colorado territories and to eke out a living as the undertaker in a town that was besieged by all types of troubles. In all of that time the one certainty had been that he did not enjoy confrontation. He did his very best to avoid it at all times, in fact.

Sometimes people change.

Slate took a quick step to the side, reached out with his left hand, and grabbed Hinder's wrist in his ghostly white hand. Hinders let out a gasp as the long fingers closed hard and squeezed. His shock became a yelp of pain as the bones in his wrist ground together. Before he could let out any other noises Slate yanked him closer. He fought. He tried to stop his forward motion, but he failed. The revolver fell from his grip as the bones in his arm broke under Slate's brutal assault.

As he opened his mouth to scream, Slate's right hand slapped him across the face hard enough to shred his lips against his teeth.

Several of the men from the bar stared on, surprised at the sudden attack. A few of them, like the bartender, took a different approach. They turned their attention from the preacher and the children to Lucas Slate.

And in the case of David Parrin, he turned his weapon in the same direction.

And through it all, Jonathan Crowley sat watching, his brown eyes looking past his rimless spectacles and focused on the bartender.

And slowly a smile spread across his face. It was not the sort of expression that offered any warmth or comfort.

Hinder let out a whimper and fell to his knees. His arm was already red and swollen, and the angry bruising was starting to show itself. The man's face was almost as pale as Slate's, and his eyes were wide and glassy.

Slate took one step and placed his foot on the fallen weapon.

He looked toward the bartender. "You planning on shooting an unarmed man?" His voice, as always, was soft, and cold.

Parrin stared at him and shook his head. "You just ruined that man."

"He was planning to kill me."

"Well, there is that." Parrin kept staring, but the amazingly large barrel of his weapon wavered a bit. "I recommend you and your friend get out of here before I decide you need killing."

It seemed a perfectly reasonable idea. He wanted to agree. Instead, however, his voice did it again. "Not going to let you hurt those children." He looked hard at the bartender. "Whatever your problem with the preacher, the children aren't a part of it."

Crowley chuckled.

Sometimes, he wanted to hurt the man.

When Crowley spoke, his voice was as calm and casual as if he were discussing the possibility of taking a stroll around the small nameless town. "I believe you'd do well to listen to Mister Slate. He can be quite unkind to people who threaten children."

The sun was gone. The world was darker than it had been only a few moments earlier and the preacher and the children were merely pools of shadow in the nighttime street.

One of the children whispered something to the preacher, but Slate couldn't hear what the little girl said. He was too busy focusing on the shotgun.

"Them children are as bad as the preacher. All of them need to be gone from this town before they drag everyone here to hell with them." Parrin's voice was remarkably calm, but his tone was hard.

Crowley sighed. "Preacher, it might be best if you took your charges back to your house for the night. Might be better to try to resolve your differences in the morning." He kept his eyes on the shadowy collection of man and children as he spoke. Though to be fair, there was some heavy doubt as to whether or not the preacher was truly a man. He looked the part, at least from a distance, but he felt wrong. He felt…vile.

"None of my flock needs worry." The preacher's voice wafted over to them, unconcerned and without any indication of stress. "Curtis and Eleanor are under my protection and the Lord shall watch out for them."

Crowley listened; his head tilted just slightly to the left. Slate listened too, and wondered at why the man's voice seemed to come from beneath something heavy as if it were muffled.

Parrin spoke up. "I told you to get out of this town and stay out, preacher!"

One of the other men took a drunken step forward. "You tell him, Davey! You make him understand he can't be here no more!"

Slate sighed. "I might be asking for your help soon, Mister Crowley."

Crowley smiled and nodded. "All you have to do is ask, Mister Slate."

Parrin pointed the shotgun at the preacher and took three steps. He was at the very edge of the porch now, and his voice carried a dangerous undercurrent. "Leave this town, preacher. No one here wants anything to do with any kind of god has anything to do with you."

Slate blinked at that. "Sounds a bit on the harsh side."

Crowley nodded. "That it does, Mister Slate. Then again, some gods are meaner than others." Damned if he did not sound amused.

The preacher spoke, "There is only one god."

Crowley snorted at the very notion.

Slate eyed the shotgun wielder. His finger was slowly squeezing down on the trigger. He was in no hurry, but Slate saw what was happening and he meant what he'd said before. He would not have the man hurting innocent children.

He reached down and plucked the Walker from under his boot.

Everyone around him was focused elsewhere it seemed, except for Hinder, who was staring at Slate with a quiet desperation. He was afraid of Slate. Part of Slate was delighted by the thought as surely as part of him was horrified by it.

The finger on the shotgun kept adding pressure.

Slate walked closer to the bartender and took careful aim. "You take your finger from that trigger, Mister Parrin, or I will be obligated to kill you."

"I'll kill them all right now if you don't back down!" Parrin's voice shook. Slate couldn't decide if it was anger or fear in that tremor.

Ultimately, he did not care. He pushed at the man and unsettled his aim.

He pulled the trigger on the Walker Colt and sent a .44 caliber charge into the bartender's skull.

Most of the bartender fell to the ground a moment later, very dead. A portion of Dave Parrin's head exploded in a crimson spray of bone and other meatier substances. Despite Slate's fears the man did not add any more pressure to the trigger of the shotgun.

"Jesus, mister, you shot Dave!" The man bellowing at him was shocked. He looked at Slate and shook, barely aware of the revolver in his hand.

Slate turned to him and leveled the barrel of the Walker in his direction. "And I'll shoot you, too, if you don't put down that revolver." His thumb pulled the hammer back to make his point. "Do you doubt me?"

There were several men looking on now and more than one of them cocked their pistols in response.

Crowley watched on silently.

The man he was aiming at very carefully raised his hands in surrender, but he did not put down the pistol.

At Slate's feet, Hinder was looking up at him with an unpleasant animal cunning in his eyes. He was likely wondering what he could do to distract Slate, to possibly aid in getting Slate's fool head blown from his shoulders.

"I don't see this going well for you, stranger." The man speaking sounded calm enough and was one of the men still aiming a weapon in his direction. "You need to surrender that piece and stand down."

Slate didn't dare look away. He had too many men looking at him with menace in their hearts.

"It seems I must ask for your assistance, Mister Crowley."

Crowley chuckled again.

And a moment later everything changed.

---

Jonathan Crowley did not move during the exchange. He sat in his chair, one hand on the mug of beer, and watched all the players. The preacher for example, did nothing while everything was happening. To be sure the children wound up behind the man's body and legs, but not because he sought to protect them. They did that by themselves.

The children looked worried, but not truly scared. They had a great deal of belief in their leader, apparently.

The herd of drunkards from the bar, on the other hand, had faith only in their numbers and their weapons. Most of them were drunk enough to be harmless at least for the moment. But that could change in an instant and it would as soon as they finished the mental arithmetic of what Slate had just done to Parrin.

Jonathan Crowley watched Slate carefully throughout the entire exchange. He liked Slate well enough, but the simple fact was that something other than human was residing inside the pale undertaker these days and that meant he had to weigh what the man did against what the entity inside him might do. He had to decide which being was in charge of that body before he made any choices regarding the man he rode with.

Currently the decision was easy enough. The man was looking out for the children. That was good enough for Crowley.

And when he asked Crowley for help, Crowley smiled.

He was more than glad to oblige.

Crowley slid from his seat in one smooth motion and reached into his coat. The reaching wasn't completely necessary, but it kept the locals calmer when his peacemakers didn't just show up out of thin air. If they could believe he had them hidden away it helped them sleep better at night. At least the ones that survived.

The men from the bar were getting properly riled up. A few of them—perhaps the ones who were most sober—were wisely backing away from the confrontation, but most were getting angrier and deadlier.

Damnedest thing, he was carrying two loaded guns and not a one of them paid him the least bit of attention. They were all, universally, focused on Lucas Slate. Granted Slate was bigger, paler, scarier and had just killed a man, but Crowley still wasn't used to the idea of not being noticed.

Three of them men finally got around to aiming their weapons. Two of them remembered to cock back the hammer beforehand, so Crowley shot them and waited on the third.

He wasn't in a killing mood, but they had to be stopped. The first one lost his pistol hand. Crowley put a hole through the man's wrist and the resulting wound took most of the flesh and bone above the targeted spot with it.

The second one took a bullet through his bicep and spun hard to the left with the impact. Both of them fell screaming.

The rest of the crowd noticed Crowley and the world felt back where it belonged.

"Fellows, I'm not much for letting anyone else get killed tonight. You should all go home." His voice came out as calm as could be, and the men looking at him noticed it. Most of them were at the edge of screaming.

"You should stay out of business that don't concern you, mister." The voice came from the back of the group. A bear of a man was coming his way and aiming a peacemaker of his own at Crowley's chest. "The preacher was warned before and both him and his children need to be gone. We don't need any strangers interfering when they don't know what is going on around here."

Crowley smiled. Most of the people on that porch flinched to see the expression on his face, but the man with the gun aimed at him did not. He might have felt a twinge of dread, but he stood his ground.

"So why don't you enlighten us? Tell us what makes the preacher so dangerous."

Slate watched both of them and shook his head, pushing the fine white hair from out of his face. The men on the porch looked back at Slate, and a few of them seemed fine with the idea of stringing him up or burning him at the stake. Crowley had seen both expressions plenty of times in his life and didn't much care for Slate's odds of walking away uninjured.

The big man looked past Crowley and down to the street, where the preacher and the children still stood.

"This doesn't concern you. That's all you need to know."

Crowley's smile grew broader on his face and the man flinched a bit. Crowley had never seen anything particularly remarkable about his smile, but he knew that others did. They found his expression unpleasant in the extreme.

"The problem here, big man, is that I am not going to leave my associate Mister Slate to handle this matter on his own, not when there are so many of you." He looked quickly. "Even after the unfortunate shots we had to make, I still count nine men on the porch to our two. And near as I can tell we are the only things stopping you and your friends from attacking a man and the two children with him."

The big man scowled. "That ain't no man. He's a demon from Hell."

Crowley's smile brightened. "I can see the confusion, but no, that man is not a demon. I'd know."

"Whatever you think he is, he can't be in this town anymore."

Crowley's smile dropped from his face and he took a step closer still to the man with the gun aimed at him. "So drag him out the right way. Get your friends and haul him to the edge of town, but Mister Slate is of the firm opinion that children should not be hurt in the process." Crowley walked closer to the gunman and stared him hard in the eyes. They were close enough to feel each other's breaths. "I share that opinion."

While the man was trying to come up with a proper response, Jonathan Crowley slapped the arm that held the gun to the side and then shoved hard at the larger man, staggering him. Before he could recover Crowley slammed into him a second time and sent him onto his backside.

The big man looked more shocked than hurt, but that expression changed over to indignation in short order.

The group of men around them began their growling all over again and Crowley ignored them. Slate was watching them already; he knew that as sure as he knew the sun had set.

"One last time, the children stay out of this or Mister Slate is unhappy. None of us wants an unhappy Mister Slate."

Slate glowered at the group of men and his voice when he spoke was as soft as ever but overflowing with menace. "I suggest you take yourselves home."

"Don't much matter anyhow. Not anymore." That came from a different source. There were two men standing on the road and looking on, watching the entire affair with worried expressions. They had every right to be worried. There were two injured men one dead man and another dozen or so with weapons in front of them.

"What do you mean it don't matter, Dirk?"

The tall man who answered was dressed in nice clothes and had shoulders about broad enough to let him pull a plow without any help from horse or ox. He bore a resemblance to their landlady and Crowley thought he saw a bit of the woman in the mannerisms of both of the men. They had the same sort of nervous smile.

"I mean the preacher's gone back to his house. Took his children with him."

"Damn it!" The big man on the ground rolled onto his knees and stood up, plucking his pistol up with him. He glared at Crowley for a moment and then looked to the two men. "When did they go?"

It was the other man who answered. The one who was likely a brother to the first. "Started walking around the same time this fella walked closer to you."

Dirk shrugged. "Guess you could still go after them if you wanted."

Big man shook his head and spit phlegm on the boards of the porch. "Guess we'll just have to wait until the next time he comes to town."

Crowley sneered. "Meaning the next time you have ten men with guns to take on one man with children?" He knew he shouldn't speak, but sometimes he couldn't resist goading on foolish people.

"Meaning you should get out of this town, mister. No one here wants you."

Crowley smiled.

The big man flinched.

Slate spoke up. "Let's just call this a done thing, Jonathan. We have no reason to offend these folks any longer."

Crowley could think of a lot of reasons, but he nodded his head.

Dirk spoke up, "Which one of you killed Dave Parrin?" His voice seemed almost too conversational, setting off warning bells in Crowley's skull.

Big man pointed at Slate. "That pale bastard did it. Shot Dave in the back of the head."

Slate nodded. "That I did. He was about to kill an unarmed man with two children. I wasn't likely to let that happen."

Crowley looked at the corpse and sighed. He'd been carrying a shotgun when he went down. Now he carried nothing at all. There was no sign of the weapon near the body.

Dirk spoke again and as he did his brother stepped around him and raised the barrel of the shotgun toward Slate's pale face. "We don't have a sheriff here. Never really needed one, but this is a safe town. I'm going to have to ask you to put down your weapon and come with me, stranger."

Slate's facial expression barely shifted at all. "And where would we be going?"

"I believe you have a room already. You'll be kept there until the morning, and after that the mayor, my father, will decide what to do with you."

Crowley looked at Slate and shrugged. "Seems like as good a place to spend the night as any other."

Several of the men in front of the bar seemed decidedly unpleased with the change. Crowley wasn't really sure why, as it was likely saving most of them from a bullet wound. He was perfectly prepared to shoot as many of the fools as necessary. He didn't much care for firearms, but he'd use them against an armed mob if he had to.

Slate nodded his head. "So let's go then."

The two brothers seemed surprised that their plan had worked.

Crowley looked at the men on the porch. "Might want to call a doctor for your friends. They're going to bleed out otherwise."

He stepped over the one he'd shot in the hand. The man flinched back as surely as if Crowley had aimed the weapon at him a second time.

A moment later they were in the street and leaving the crowd of men behind. He could see the big man looking at the ruined hand of one of his victims.

"You planning on shooting anyone?" Dirk's voice was calm, he was looking at Crowley.

"Not at the moment, no."

"Then you might want to put those away."

A simple gesture and the weapons faded away into the place where Crowley hid them. "Put what away?"

Dirk snorted. The other one laughed. "Neat trick."

"Robert, now is not the time."

Robert shook his head. "We did what Mother said and we got the men. What better time?"

Slate's cold, soft whisper came between the two brothers. "Gentlemen, if you could explain what's going on here, we'd be obliged."

Dirk spoke up as they walked toward the hotel. "Mostly what's going on here is we thought you should have a chance to walk away without getting shot up. The boys at the bar might be drunk but they aren't so far gone they couldn't find you to shoot. And there were a lot of them."

Robert laughed again. Crowley decided he liked the man.

"There's more to it than that." Much as he often preferred to stay quiet, the situation was annoying Crowley. "What did the preacher do to get half the people in your town ready to string him up?"

"He's stayed away from my family so far, but we keep hearing stories. People saying he does magic. Saying he's stealing people's souls."

Crowley looked to the man and studied his face. He seemed perfectly sincere. "Stealing souls? Really? And how does he do that?"

"Well, I have never actually seen him do any such thing and he seems to be helping those children he's with, but as half of them came here with him and the rest were orphaned after he came to town, it's hard to say what's the truth."

Slate looked at the revolver in his hand and shook his head. Crowley suspected he was wondering about the man he'd killed. "There have been a lot of deaths since he came here?"

Robert responded. "Yes sir. There have. There've been about ten that I can think of." He paused. "Eleven if you count Dave back there."

Slate shook his head. "He wasn't giving me much choice."

"No one's going to hold that against you. Not really. Dave charged too much for his bad liquor anyways." Crowley looked at the man again. He seemed very casual about the death of a town member.

"So then why are we under arrest?"

Dirk answered. "You're not. Not really. We just needed to get you away from those folk so we could ask for your help."

"Our help?" Crowley felt his skin tighten a bit.

"Isn't that how this works, Mister Crowley? Don't people have to ask for your help before they get it?"

Crowley's smile came back. "How would you know about that?"

"My father says he's met you before. A while back, in Boston."

Crowley nodded his head, curious now. He hadn't been to Boston in several years.

---

# Part Four: The House Of The Lord

Crowley and Slate walked slowly from the inn and looked along the nearly empty streets of the nameless town, both of them somber. There was a time for jesting and that time was past.

The night before, Lucas Slate had killed a man, pulled a trigger and fired a very large bullet into the back of the man's head, nearly removing his face completely in the process. The man had been preparing to kill a preacher and two children. From what they'd heard the death of the preacher might well have been justified, but the children? That was something Slate would not condone.

"How long since you've been to Boston, Mister Crowley?"

"Well, it's been a good long while, Mister Slate."

Walter Perry, the man who was the de facto mayor of the nameless town, had been very surprised to see Jonathan Crowley. He had also been deeply shocked that the man was not at least thirty or more years older. The last time Walter Perry had seen Lucas Slate's companion he had been seven years of age.

That had been a long while back, well over thirty years.

Slate looked at his companion and nodded. That was about the answer he'd expected from the man. Jonathan Crowley seldom gave a straight answer to any of the questions that mattered. He could never decide if there was a legitimate reason for the man's reticence or if it merely amused him.

The stretch of dirt they walked down—which was also the closest thing to a main street in the town—was uneven and dusty. The air smelled of the promise of rain, but so far there were no clouds worth noticing and the dust was still doing its best to coat everything.

So they saw the mob coming their way without any trouble at all. Some of the faces were familiar from the night before, but now they were sober, better armed and in the company of many more like-minded individuals.

"Hey!" He recognized the speaker immediately; the night before Slate'd done his level best to break the man's arm. Instead, he'd just caused all kinds of ruination on the fool's wrist. Hinder was up and about; his right wrist bound heavily in cloth strips and wooden splints. His face was pale and dark rings surrounded his eyes, but he was up and he was angry.

Crowley smiled and touched the brim of his gambler's hat. "Good morning, Mister Hinder. How's that arm of yours?" His voice was civilized with just a tinge of contempt to make sure everyone knew his opinion of the man he spoke to.

"My problem is with you and your friend. You killed a good man last night."

"Which one?"

"What?" Hinder looked unsettled by the question.

"The fellow I shot in the wrist? He died last night. Bled out before anyone could patch him up." Crowley's voice remained calm and almost cheery. "Pity about that, but he drew on me first."

Hinder's face reddened and he stomped a foot. Perhaps it was the closest he could come to a tantrum when one considered the pain he was in.

"You two bastards need to leave this town right now!" His face had color again as he roared his demand.

Crowley shook his head.

"Can't leave yet. Got to deal with the preacher."

"We'll take care of the preacher on our own, mister. Just like you suggested." He nodded to the man on his left. The fellow was very large, not muscular, just extremely heavy, but he had a length of thick rope wrapped several times around his arm and draped like a toga over his barrel chest.

Slate's mouth did it again, opening and speaking before he could stop it. "And the children with the preacher?"

"They'll get what they have coming."

Slate's lips pulled down in a silent scowl. He felt it, but did not stop it.

Right next to him, Crowley's lips peeled up into a truly frightening smile.

"Well now," Crowley purred. "You can touch those children just as soon as you're done dealing with me and my companion. And I assure you, Mister Slate is more frightening than he looks."

Slate let the insult go. It was best not to fall for Crowley's comments.

Hinder took a step forward and spat.

"Guess we'll have to deal with you first then."

Hinder was not carrying a weapon. The same could not be said for the small army of men around him. The sound of weapons being readied was one Jonathan Crowley was all too familiar with.

"We aren't alone, you know." Crowley spoke softly, but everyone heard him.

"Yeah? Who else you have with you?" Hinder sounded very cocky.

"Well, that would be Walter Perry and his two sons, Dirk and Robert." Crowley nodded his head to the left and indicated where the three men were standing. All of them were armed, too. "I have been asked to handle the preacher so many of you have a problem with and to try to save the children in the process. That is exactly what I intend to do." Crowley stayed where he was, not making any sudden moves. "And I intend to take care of the matter now. Should you attempt to interfere with me, gentlemen, I will consider you my enemies."

He stared hard at Hinder. Hinder tried to stare hard back, but after a few seconds he looked down at the ground.

"If I haven't handled your problem by this evening, you can take matters into your own hands, but the man most of you call the mayor has asked for my help and I intend to give it. Do not make me consider you my enemies. You will not appreciate the trouble that causes you."

Hinder glared with as much venom as he could manage. The effect was lost on Crowley, who once again started walking toward the whitewashed house that served as a church for the towering stranger he'd seen the night before.

The preacher, who apparently took care of many an orphaned child, and who, according to some of the townsfolk, was responsible for them becoming orphans.

Hinder's mouth opened and closed, a few indignant noises coming from it, but no truly noteworthy sounds. All around him the crowd fell apart, heading in their different directions.

Crowley allowed himself a small smile that was seen by no one but Slate. The man knew exactly what was going through Crowley's mind because he had said it at on at least a dozen occasions, usually while they ate a meal at the end of a long day's riding. *There are two types of people, Mister Slate. There are wolves and there are sheep. Find the wolves, take away their fangs, and the sheep will move off on their own and cause no harm.*

It would have been easy to take offense at the tone or the comment, but Slate knew better. Crowley was merely stating what he considered an elemental truth. So far Slate had found no true flaw with the philosophy and it wasn't for lack of trying.

The rest of their walk was uneventful, and Slate considered the conversation with the founding family of the town. Crowley was a known quantity to the father of the Perry clan. They had met long ago. He remembered Crowley clearly and eyed the man with a bit of fear and a healthy apprehension. As far as Slate was concerned men should not move through the years without aging.

Then again, he seldom even had to shave these days and his body kept changing, so who was he to judge?

"How do you plan to handle this, Mister Crowley?"

Crowley looked his way and that small smirk that so often passed for his smile crept across his mouth for a moment. "I believe I will ask the preacher a few questions. From there we shall see what happens."

There might have been a few people that thought the man was in a joking mood, but Slate knew better. Crowley was not the sort who liked to go into any situation without first knowing who or what he was dealing with.

What they knew for certain was that there was something odd about the preacher's face, that he had come to the town only a few months earlier, that he took care of orphans and that a goodly number of the local folk admired him and twice as many saw him coming and found a better place to be.

The preacher did not carry a gun. He did not believe in weapons other than those provided by the Lord. According to several second-hand accounts, he also did not need them.

They walked slowly toward the white structure at the edge of the small town. Beyond it the river meandered through the area. They had bathed in those very waters when they arrived in town and had done so in the shadow of the white house that was used as the preacher's church, though it bore no cross. That house was not natural. It squatted in the ground like a toadstool, bloated and poisonous, though most could not have seen that particular fact. Most were not prepared to see it, and even if they were, did not have the right eyes for the job.

Slate had the right eyes. He suspected Crowley did as well, though the man never said as much.

The place was as dark as Slate remembered. It was painted a white that fairly radiated in the early morning sunlight but still it seemed locked in shadows.

Jonathan Crowley's smiled faded away as he stared at the structure.

In front of and around the building was the congregation, a large gathering of folks for so small a town. Men and women, a few young adults, but mostly children ranging from the age of three up into the late teens. The people were dressed in their finest clothes. They were silent as the men approached, all save the children, who softly broke into a blasphemous hymn when they saw Crowley and Slate.

The words did not make sense, but they made Slate's skin crawl.

Crowley slowed down his strides and tilted his head just a bit to the left as if listening to something other than the words. Whenever he did that sort of thing, Slate wanted to walk the other way.

"What are you—?"

Crowley held up a hand and silenced him with the gesture. The children kept singing.

Crowley gathered a handful of dirt from the ground and cupped it in his palm as the children's voices rose in a sweet, unnatural chorus.

And then Crowley spoke into his palm and dropped the dirt.

By all the laws of nature that dirt should have fallen straight down and mingled with the rest of the dust on the road. Instead, it drifted on the air currents and then merged with the air itself until it was gone.

And one moment after that the children started coughing harsh, barking noises as they gagged on nothing and choked on air.

"Well then, that's settled." Crowley nodded to himself and walked forward again.

"What the hell did you do?"

Crowley looked his way. "I made them stop singing."

"Fair enough."

Crowley looked at the people around the children. Most of them simply stared, not even considering offering their aid. The coughing fit had not abated. The youths were still coughing and gagging.

"And did you plan to let them breathe properly again, Mister Crowley?"

"Just as soon as I am certain they'll stop singing any songs."

Two of the children fell to the ground, gasping and red-faced. Another looked on the verge of fainting. The rest continued to cough, but three were no longer afflicted by their coughing fits. Slate watched on until most of the children had had collapsed.

Crowley continued to watch the adults around them. The adults looked about as if seeking guidance.

"Is it possible that they're as stupid as all that?" Crowley's smile was gone and he kept studying the adults.

"It is indeed, Mister Crowley."

"Preacher! You should come out here. We need to have a talk." When Crowley bellowed the adults around him flinched as if he'd threatened them.

"He won't come. He's sleeping." The man who spoke was young, but looked older because of his shoddy clothes and the dirt crusted into his skin.

Crowley stared at him for a second. "Well. Why don't you go wake the man?"

"Not a chance, mister. I'd rather not die today."

"You here because you believe what the preacher says? Or are you here because you're afraid?"

The man looked away from Crowley and down to the ground, answering the question without any words.

"Mister Slate?"

"Yes, Mister Crowley?"

"I believe it's time to remove this particular blight."

"And how do you propose to do that?"

Crowley looked at his hand for a moment and made a fist. When his hand opened again a blossom of flames was settled in the palm. It did not burn Crowley's flesh but was bright enough to be seen past the glare of the morning sun.

Slate nodded his head and raised the shotgun he was carrying. He aimed toward the sky and pulled the trigger. The thunder that erupted was enough to catch the attention of every man, woman and child.

"I believe it is time for all of you to leave this place." His voice was as soft as ever. Everyone listened just the same.

Most of the adults started heading away and Crowley shook his head. "Take the children with you."

"Ain't my kids." The woman who spoke was rail thin, stoop shouldered and in desperate need of a bath.

Crowley smiled at her and she flinched back from him. "Do I need to repeat myself?"

"No sir." She moved toward the children, helping a few of them to their feet.

"What were those children singing, Mister Crowley?" Slate spoke as the adults ushered the young ones away from the white building. Several of the children actually started crying as they were taken away from the place and a few actually tried to head back in that direction. The skinny woman was smart enough to know that was a bad idea and barked orders at a couple of people who helped her herd them away.

"There are words that have power and there are songs that have power. I have no idea what they were saying, which means it is likely something the local people might have spoken in the past."

"But you stopped them anyway?"

"How did that song make you feel, Mister Slate?"

"Like my skin wanted to hide itself under the ground."

"That is reason enough for me."

"I do not know what they were singing, Mister Crowley, but I suspect if I wanted to know, I could learn the meanings easily enough."

"And that is why we are still riding together, Mister Slate. Because you have something inside of you that is as foreign to me as their words and I don't like mysteries I cannot solve."

Crowley looked at the building again.

"Preacher! You have one minute before I burn your house down around you!" Despite his words, Crowley threw the contents of his hand at the whitewashed house. The flames licked at the side of the building and blazed, but the wood did not burn and the paint did not blacken.

Slate looked at that for a moment and then looked at Crowley. "Well now, that is something you seldom see."

"Not everything is as it appears, Mister Slate."

Something inside the white building made a noise that was not human and never had been. The same sound was echoed from the other side of town, on the road leading toward the nameless gathering place.

"What made that noise?" Slate stared off into the distance.

"Do you remember the figure we saw when we approached town, Mister Slate? The scarecrow?"

"Is that what it was?" He nearly shivered. The scarecrow was a collection of animal bones wrapped in baked mud and surrounded by a tattered cloak. It had been unpleasant to look at in the extreme.

"Probably not, but it certainly had similar purposes, I expect."

"What purpose is that?"

From the distance, clear on the other side of town, they heard screams.

Crowley looked in that direction. "To scare off pests."

"And are we scared then, Mister Crowley?"

"Moderately apprehensive, Mister Slate." Crowley looked his way and his smile was back. He was excited. This was what he lived for much as he refused to admit it. He loved the danger and the risk and the unknown things he encountered. "Would you rather handle the scarecrow? Or the preacher?"

"I believe I shall investigate your scarecrow, Mister Crowley."

"Delightful. I'll wait here. I expect the preacher will be with me sooner rather than later."

Slate nodded his head and turned back the way they'd come. There was something in the road at the far side of town, a dark shape that was moving in their direction. Whatever it was, it roared as it came closer.

Lucas Slate looked at his shotgun and then at that shape and doubted the weapon would do him the least bit of good.

The preacher rose from his bed and reached for his mask. He could not be seen without it. That would be to show too much to the people who were not yet ready to accept their Lord and Savior.

Far away the Guardian responded to his call with one of its own, and then came toward him. Beneath him, the house, his church, was suffering. He felt its pain and knew that it would not survive if he did not do something about the man screaming for his attention. The building would not look harmed to the unwary, but he could feel the flames eating at the side of the building, growing stronger with each passing minute.

The children were silenced and that filled the preacher with a deep and abiding anger.

Somewhere within the preacher's heart a brief flash of savage joy came at the thought that he might be stopped or slowed down. The thought came from the body, of course, from the human being who had once been in charge of the form. Daniel Murdock had not given his body freely. He still fought and tried to hold onto the flesh that he had been born into. No matter how hard the preacher tried he could not remove the last vestiges of the man's personality. Still, at most the man's memories were like a bothersome tooth. An ache, yes, an inconvenience, but not enough to stop him.

The mask slid onto his face and he felt the wood and leather grip his skull and pull in closer. His eyes opened and saw.

He stood and looked down. The two men from the day before were down there. The gaunt and ghostly one was walking away. The other, the grinning fool, was looking up at his window and smiling all the broader. There was something about that man that he did not like and did not trust.

Killing him would eliminate the problem.

---

Crowley stared at the house that was not a house for a long while, fully aware that something that was no longer mud and bones and tattered cloth was heading toward him and that the only thing between him and that particular nightmare was Lucas Slate.

That was all right. He wanted to see what Slate could do on his own.

The house was diseased. He knew that. He had known it the first time he saw it. What he'd wanted to see more was whether or not his companion noticed, and he did.

There weren't many things Crowley could do without being asked to help. He could defend himself; he could certainly observe to his heart's content. He could make comments. But he had a great deal of power and that power had severe limitations that were there to prevent him becoming anything at all like the creatures he fought. Or like what he suspected Slate was becoming.

He pushed the notion aside and focused on the building. He could feel the damage his little spell had done and was continuing to do. As bad as the church was, as much as he felt the cancerous structure's potential for causing trouble, the man inside was the major threat.

He needed taking care of.

"Come outside, preacher. This is the last warning." He did not draw his weapons. Guns, he suspected, would do little good in any event.

The preacher came to the door and stepped out into the morning light. Somewhere under the man's hat his eyes were probably squinting at the morning glare, but it was impossible to tell for certain because of the growth covering his face.

Crowley let himself see with human eyes for only a moment, and saw the face of a human man. He was pleasant enough and kept a well-trimmed beard and a thin mustache on his broad face.

But when Crowley looked at him with his attention properly focused, he saw the leather and wood that had been carved to look like a human face. The angles were the same, and there was horsehair sewn onto the dark leather to mimic the beard and mustache of the human face. But that was as close to human as the mask got. Dark pits revealed nothing but shadows where the eyes should have been and the mouth of the mask hung open like a dead man's slack, gaping maw. The nose was only a jutting piece of leather covering a rough wooden shape. The leather of the mask intertwined with raw, bleeding flesh and gripped the back of the head with tongues of bloodied sinew and thread.

Under that mask, something was waiting, hidden from sight and convinced, no doubt, that anyone seeing it would see only a man.

"You are welcome here, stranger, if you seek the comfort of the Lord, our God."

"Which god is that?" Crowley didn't even try to keep the humor from his voice.

"There is only one God."

"Indeed? And what is that god's name?"

It was a simple question and if the man were a preacher in the traditional sense, he'd have one of several possible answers.

"Come inside and we can discuss this."

Crowley shook his head.

"I don't think that would work out the way you want it to."

"Stranger, you have taken the devoted from my side and you try to drive me from my home." The preacher's voice was remarkably calm, though if Crowley listened the right way he could hear other sounds beyond the noise of a human speaking English. They were not good sounds. "If you seek to anger me, I am not easily angered. If you seek to wound me, I am protected by the Lord. If you seek to find comfort and salvation you have come to the right place, but if you seek anything else, you are wasting both my time and yours."

Crowley listened to the words and shook his head. "Honestly? You talk too damned much."

He took four fast, hard strides toward the preacher and grabbed his mask as quickly as he could. The man let out a surprised gasp and then screamed in shock as his face was ripped away.

Crowley hurled the mask into the street behind him and looked at the preacher.

There was a dark pit where the skull of the man should have been and he could see long, spindly limbs holding onto the sides of the fleshy wound. They were mottled in spots of yellow and black and a faded peach hue.

"What the hell are you?" Crowley stared intently, wondering what the answer would be.

Sometimes he loved his job.

———

Lucas Slate saw the thing coming and barely recognized it. He looked away long enough to reload his weapon, flinching inside as he did. The scarecrow outside of the town had been smaller, and, well, mostly just mud and bones. This thing had a proper face, with very large teeth and a few tusks, besides. It also had flesh of sorts, though to be kind, the flesh was sagging and gelid. The entire affair shook with each stride it took, and the hands on the brute were as large as his horse's head. Sadly, they suited the rest of the nightmare's size.

The creature stank of decay and a heavy swarm of blowflies swept around it. Somewhere along the way the hood had fallen back and he saw more of the face than he wanted to. The uneven head, the bloated eyes as pale as his own. Nothing about the creature was pleasant.

The thing stopped and looked at him and then let out a roar loud enough to shake the clothes on his body.

Apparently it felt the same way about him.

"Weren't you supposed to come to my assistance, Mister Crowley?" he asked, knowing full well he would not get an answer.

It charged.

Slate raised his shotgun and waited a few more paces. When he could feel the ground shaking under the monster's tread, he aimed the weapon and fired both barrels.

Portions of the thing blew away in a double roar of thunder and the thing staggered and fell back a moment. One side of the chest was opened all the way through and Slate could see rotten entrails hiding inside that torso. They did not make sense and they most assuredly were not in any particular order. As a mortician with a long history, he would have known.

Without waiting to see if the thing would attack again, he drew his revolver and fired as quickly as he could until the weapon was empty. Hole after hole exploded through the creature's chest and dropped more rotten meat onto the street. The flies around the gory mess buzzed ecstatically.

As the thing was looking at him with a malignant eye, Slate was not as pleased as the flies.

It charged again and Slate felt that change take place within him.

He did not want the change, but some things were beyond his control.

Whatever it was that inhabited his body and was making the changes in him intended to stay alive and defend itself. His foot rose and came down hard upon the dry street and the ground from his heel to the monster split itself violently, shaking the buildings around him and sending several onlookers to their knees or their backsides. Most of the people watching were from the congregation of the church and the adults looked terrified. The children looked...angry.

The thing coming at him was in midstride when the earth split wide beneath it. It had enough time to let out another roar before falling into the pit and vanishing from sight. An instant later the ground slammed itself back together, leaving a very visible scar where the scarecrow beast had been.

Whatever had flared to life inside of Slate was not yet done, however, and where he'd hoped that the odd sensation that showed itself when the thing attacked might have faded away, it remained, singing in his nerves and buzzing in his brain.

---

The preacher, what was left of him at any rate, turned its hollow face toward Crowley and swung one powerful arm. Crowley stepped back and blocked the blow, felt the impact run through his wrist and elbow and staggered back a bit. The faceless thing hit like a mule kicks. Unfortunately, Crowley had experience with that particular sensation.

The preacher spoke to him, a flow of low grunts and syllables that made no sense to him. He'd learned many of the languages from the Indians that lived in the Americas but whatever it said was little more than gibberish.

"Try it in English, you damned thing." He stepped forward and drove his fist into the hole where the preacher's face had been, doing his best not to think about the depth his hand entered. His knuckles contacted something hard and he felt what might have been teeth brush across his fingers even as he delivered the blow.

The preacher stepped back, a wet, bleating noise escaping its cavernous face.

Somewhere in the distance something violent happened and the buildings around him shuddered. There were a couple of shacks that fell apart, but the church remained undamaged, and even the widows didn't vibrate with the heavy shaking.

The preacher screamed again and fell to his knees in the dust. Crowley would have been happier about it if he'd been the one to cause the sudden change in the man's demeanor, but he knew better.

For a moment he thought the preacher might be sick. Instead, the man's body grew rigid and then something started vomiting from the hole where his face should have been.

At that exact moment, the children started their damned singing again and Crowley felt the fine hairs on his arms rise even through his clothing.

Dark magics indeed, though they felt completely unfamiliar.

Long, spider-like legs crept from the face of the preacher and found purchase in the dirt, growing visibly longer and thicker as they touched the earth. Each of the limbs ended in a series of curved barbs that sank into the earth even as the preacher reared back like a startled horse and more of whatever the hell was inside of him pulled free from his hollow body.

Behind that thing, Lucas Slate was coming his way and sporting an expression that had nothing at all to do with his companion's usual demeanor.

"Lucas! Stay back!"

Slate did not listen. He came forward, his hands curled into tight fists and his teeth bared in a snarl of hatred.

And when he spoke the words were all too similar to the sounds coming from the thing that crawled from the preacher's insides.

And the children's sweet voices sang out in the same unknown language.

Madness. Crowley felt his grin spreading across his face and tried to decide which threat to take care of first.

Whatever the children were doing, it was connected and he wanted it to stop. Once more he grabbed a handful of dirt and cast it into the air, muttering his own words. The dust vanished even as it streaked like a dozen dirty comets toward each of the children. Only a second later they were once again coughing and staggering, incapable of continuing their songs.

Slate looked his way with unfamiliar eyes. There was none of the usual quiet humor or kindness to be seen in the man's demeanor. He considered Crowley only for a moment before he turned toward the preacher and the thing crawling from him.

Crowley eyed that nightmare too. It had grown, and Crowley looked at it with utter disgust. Had he thought it looked remotely like a spider? He was wrong. Closer, perhaps to a centipede. The long limbs he saw numbered well into the dozens and possibly as many as a hundred. The body kept spilling out, a black, glossy, chitinous shape mottled with colors and covered in rotting meat. Whatever the preacher had been, if he had ever been human, was quickly rotting now that the thing inside it was slipping free.

And the head of the thing? Well, that was just possibly the worst of it. There were a great number of uneven eyes and there was something remotely like a nose and below that were black petals of sharp, hard blades and a gaping maw that pulsated at the center of the flowering blades.

It made a sound, a mewling, wailing noise and it rose into the air, easily fifteen feet long and still slithering from the preacher.

Crowley tried to think of anything he could do to hurt it and the first thing that came to mind was his guns. He might not like them, but he liked the idea of touching that thing even less.

Lucas Slate barked out harsh words and the thing crawling from the preacher looked his way and let out a warbling shriek.

Crowley took aim at the thing, trying to decide which misshapen eye to hit first, and Slate strode directly to the thing and grabbed the vulgar head of the bug in both of his hands.

It shrieked and raised a dozen of its long limbs. They reared back and the three claws at the end of each foot of the thing spread, the better to sink into Slate's body.

Instead Slate opened his mouth very wide and breathed out, a powerful gust of something white that wrapped around the head of the creature like steam but clung like thick cobwebs.

Slate jumped back, clearing almost fifteen feet in one bound. He landed and slid a few more feet, managing to keep his balance. His face looked wrong in that moment, less like a man and more like something else.

The thing still crawling from the preacher's body was easily forty feet in length and as thick around as Crowley's thigh, but it still kept spilling out, like a snake that managed to hide inside a box too small to hold it.

It let out another sound, different this time, higher and more desperate, and flung itself back, its long limbs trying to pull at whatever wrapped around its head. Instead of tugging the stuff free, the limbs turned white and withered as they entered the odd wisps. He could not see the face of the thing through whatever was covering its head but if the same thing was happening inside of that caul, it would not last much longer.

It stopped screaming and fell back, the entire body shuddering and thrashing across the street.

As Crowley watched the mottled body grew white. The shell of the thing split as it changed color and stranger things still spilled out from inside it.

The putrefying body of the preacher convulsed, too, and bucked and thrashed and kicked madly as the thing continued to vomit out from inside the ruined head.

The children were choking and coughing on his spell, but something else was happening too. The coughing dust should have left them uncomfortable, but no more. Now they fell to the ground as well, and like the preacher they thrashed and spasmed. And from somewhere inside of them something mewled and called in a cacophony of voices that were too familiar for comfort.

Part of Jonathan Crowley wanted to help the children, but he knew it was too late. They, like the preacher, were either already dead or in the process of becoming something else. Whatever had been in the preacher had done what all life does. It had gone forth and multiplied.

One by one the children stopped moving. As they did, the sounds they made faltered and failed. Their skin grew white and split and what was inside of them rolled out in a slurry of rot.

And Crowley watched. Made himself watch. Because to do less was to do them an injustice and to risk forgetting why he fought the nightmares that hid among people.

The preacher finally stopped moving. His body collapsed on itself like a rotted gourd.

Lucas Slate let out a moan and fell to his hands and knees.

Jonathan Crowley turned to look at the church of the devoted and found that it too was rotting now and the flames he'd cast upon it were doing their job and burning what did not decompose. He looked down at the mask the preacher had worn and it was lifeless, nothing but a collection of leather and wood. The leather, he saw, had once bound a book. He could just make out the faded words *Holy Bible* in the grain of the material. Just the same, he put four holes into the thing and blew it to pieces. Better to be overly cautious. He'd learned that a long while back. After he made sure none of the parts tried to do anything suspicious, he turned back to his companion.

He took Slate's arm and helped him to his feet. The mortician's mind was once again his, by all appearances.

They walked slowly and Crowley took the time to pick up Slate's weapons.

"Just what was that, Mister Slate?"

"Do you mean the thing that crawled out of the preacher or do you mean my reaction to it?" Slate's voice, always as quiet as the grave, was softer even than usual. His southern drawl was, for the moment, far more pronounced. A sign that he was as stressed as he looked.

"Both I suppose."

"I am afraid my answer in both cases remains exactly the same, Mister Crowley. I do not know." He stood a little straighter and stretched his neck. The adults among the devoted looked around in confusion. The children were little more than small corpses rotting away in clothes that remained dirtied but intact.

"Is this a victory then, Mister Crowley?"

Crowley looked around and shook his head. The house let out a sigh and a moan and crumbled in a dry heap. "Not to my way of reckoning, Mister Slate. But then I can seldom claim that I have seen a proper victory. Most occasions I'd call it an uneven draw."

They headed for the center of town and for their rooms and their horses. There was no longer a reason to stay. Whatever had inhabited the preacher was gone and from what the townsfolk had said it come to the town with him from somewhere else.

The townsfolk did a spectacular job of pretending not to notice them as they headed for the mercantile and inn. Even the ones who had asked for their help in the first place. That suited Crowley just fine. He preferred to avoid complications and gratitude from strangers was little more than a complication in his eyes.

"We're going to ride, Mister Slate. Tomorrow or the day after, we'll discuss what happened in greater detail."

"I expect I'll be ready by then. Just for the present, I need to gather my thoughts." The man did not look at Crowley as he spoke.

For a time they rode in silence. It was not the comfortable silence they had shared on their way into the nameless town.

# White Blank Page (Songs in the Key of White)

Lucas Slate sat astride his dark horse and stared into the sprawling affair with little or no expression on his gaunt face. He looked upon the collection of hastily assembled buildings and well-used tents with eyes half-lidded. An unwary sort of soul might have thought he wasn't paying attention, but he was.

"It occurs to me, Mister Crowley, that this place looks too much like other areas we've both seen in the past."

The air had a hard bite to it. The wind was dry and cold and cutting. Winter was well and properly on its way and the people in the small town knew it. They were shilling their goods with a sort of cheerful desperation that said at least a few of them could think of better places to be. He wondered if any of them would succeed in finding those better places before the winter came properly.

Jonathan Crowley, who was riding his own horse and sitting only a few feet from Slate, allowed himself a small smile and shook his head. "And, what, exactly, is it that you think we're going to find here, Mister Slate?"

Slate did not bother turning to the sound of Crowley's voice. He knew what he would see. The same lean, plain features and brown hair, brown eyes. Same offensive smirk on the man's longish face, though at the moment it was hidden behind almost a month's worth of beard growth. They'd ridden across half the Arizona territory because something inside of Lucas Slate told him he had to be here, but he had no idea what that something was.

He just knew it chewed at him.

Only a short time ago he'd been quite a different man. His hair white, and his skin was as pale as snow, same as always. He was an albino, after all. But beyond that there was remarkably little that was the same.

When he'd lived in Carson's Point, Colorado he'd stood at least eight inches shorter and he'd been told more than once that he had the face of a woman. True, a few of the folks who'd made that claim had been drunk and desperately lonely, but he knew that his face had been different, as surely as his body had changed.

Slate stood over six feet in height now, and while he still sported the same hat he'd taken to wearing as the local undertaker—a fine old hat that served him well and looked somber enough for funerals—he could no longer fit in his old suits and had been forced to buy new shirts and new pants as well; rawhide in this case because the damnable cold would have sunk through anything less.

He had always been thin. Now he was gaunt, and his muscles were cords of leather under skin that had long since stopped being supple and soft. No one would ever mistake him for a woman these days. Instead, they'd contemplate whether or not someone sharing his old profession should have buried him. He was not dead. He just looked the part.

He had always been soft spoken, but these days his voice was lower and seldom seemed to want to come out as much more than a whisper. The only thing that had not changed was the cultured southern drawl that moved through his words. "I'm intending to find answers, Mister Crowley."

Crowley nudged his horse closer. He looked toward the man and considered the beard he was growing. Jonathan Crowley did not look like a man who should have a beard to him. It didn't seem to fit his long face. "I am very fond of answers, Mister Slate. But I have to ask, what, exactly, is the question?"

He looked at Crowley. The man was dressed in fine clothes. A cotton shirt, a charcoal, pinstriped suit with a vest, and over that a great duster that kept the cold and wind from touching anything under it. He sported a gambler's hat on the top of his head, and a heavy wool scarf of a dark, somber red hue.

Slate offered a thin-lipped smile of his own. "I believe the question is the very one you've been contemplating since we started riding together. What, exactly, am I becoming?"

Crowley nodded his head. "That is a question worth answering."

"Indeed it is, sir."

---

You could hardly call it a town, really. More a collection of shops and brothels all shoved together and becoming a town already called Silver Springs, Arizona. The place was a collection of thieves and whores and criminals, as could be expected in a boomtown. The rumors of silver had driven herds of people into the area and the fortunate few who had struck solid claims guaranteed they'd stay. There were white folk, red folk and black folk, all of them in the same area. He imagined if he looked around he'd even see a few Chinese as well. That seldom happened in places that were properly called civilized. There were too many who considered the other races as enemies for that. Here, where money was more important than opinions, there was less need of being selective.

Crowley rather liked that part of the situation. He'd never much cared for the need to believe one people were better than another. One on one, most of them seemed all right. It was only when you gathered any of them in groups they tended to be stupid.

The ground was as dry as the air, which is to say most of the folks in the area would be getting their water from wells, or from the barrels a few enterprising people were bringing with them. It was a commodity. The Verde River was a few hours ride from the area, and he had already seen a group of men at the edge of town working on figuring the best way to get the water from there to here. What they lacked in equipment they seemed to make up for with enthusiasm.

He could see that Lucas Slate was tense. Slate, who seldom seemed bothered by much of anything since he'd begun changing. Slate, who calmly and methodically followed through with some very grisly work, was currently as taut as a bowstring.

"We have traveled through Indian territories and been shot at several times, Mister Slate. Who do you think is most likely to be of assistance to us in this situation?"

The two of them were still at the edge of the crowded area. Someone, somewhere, had claimed they found silver in the area. A week later the first building seemed old. Now? Now the crowds kept coming and the buildings kept popping up like mushrooms after a rainstorm.

Slate looked slowly over the area and then finally shook his head. "I'm sure I have no idea."

Crowley smiled. "Look around us, Mister Slate, and tell me what's different about the people here?"

"Nothing that I can see." He spoke even as he once more scanned the crowds. "Ah. I see it now."

"What do you see, Mister Slate?"

"The Indians. They're more afraid of *me* than they are of *you*."

Crowley chuckled. "Well now, don't you think that deserves a bit of investigation?"

Slate took off his hat for a moment and ran long, pallid fingers through his long, thin, white hair. "Indeed I do, Mister Crowley. Indeed I do."

They rode forward at a leisurely pace, two men who scared most people without even trying.

---

Silver Springs wasn't old enough to be on any maps. The town had been hastily assembled and that tended to make navigating the structures challenging. There were no rules, really, except the ones people managed to force on each other. Most of the folks who saw the strangers eyed them warily, rather like one might contemplate a substantial rattlesnake that was minding its own affairs but was looking at you with one ophidian eye.

To be fair they struck quite a few notes that qualified them as unusual. The gaunt man rode on a pale grey horse that didn't seem to breathe. It did not snort, nor did it whinny. The beast seemed oblivious to most of the other animals in the area, though the same was not true in reverse. A good number of dogs made it a point to be elsewhere when the horse got too close, and they made certain to bark their dissatisfaction just as soon as they were far enough away to assure the great horse could not easily get to them.

The man riding with him seemed of particularly good humor, with an eager smile that did not sit well. More than a few of the faithful crossed themselves when they saw his broad, even teeth. When Crowley was not smiling he was hardly remarkable, but there was something inherently wrong with his grin. There was something about the way he moved, the way he looked at folks, that left them a mite worried that he could just possibly take note of them. His horse was only remarkable in that it did not run from the larger grey beast the gaunt man rode.

Both men sported weapons, but that was hardly unusual in this area. The gaunt man had a long rifle draped across his saddle, held in place by the weight of his hands. A shotgun rested near his leg, and a careful eye would make out the two Colt Navy revolvers tucked into saddle holsters. And knives? There was a knife hilt at the top of each boot and at least one large blade strapped to his hip. He carried enough weapons to promise mayhem, even if his deathlike face and grim pallor hadn't already advertised a penchant for destruction.

Crowley slipped off his horse with an unsettling grace. He didn't bother stretching or adjusting his posture as so many did. Instead, he seemed perfectly relaxed and comfortable. Lucas Slate dropped down with substantially more difficulty and looked around the area with hooded eyes.

"You're not feeling well, Mister Slate?"

"Something's wrong. I don't quite know what, or why, but I'm feeling decidedly ill at ease."

Jonathan Crowley adjusted his wide brimmed gambler's hat and looked around carefully. "In the time I've known you I've run across remarkably little that put you under the weather."

"Indeed, sir. It is a rarity." Slate's soft southern drawl was more pronounced. "And one I daresay I do not enjoy."

"Close your eyes, Mister Slate."

The man did as Crowley suggested.

"Now, tell me what you feel both in your body and outside it."

To most, the conversation would have seemed foolish, but Lucas Slate knew better. He was changing and his changes included some very devilish alterations to his senses. He could often see past the lies that presented themselves to most people, and he could occasionally feel much more than he should have been able to consider.

"Well now..."

Crowley said nothing, but he watched the man very carefully.

Slate turned his head slowly to the left and tilted his ear higher, as if trying to catch a sound. "Well now," he repeated. "That's something, isn't it?"

"What might that be, Mister Slate?"

"I can hear something. Sounds almost like music, but nothing that makes sense."

Crowley nodded his head slowly. All around them people were going on about their business and giving a wide berth to the two of them. "Then I might suggest you investigate. Shall I come with you?" He made the offer already knowing the answer.

"Not at this time, Mister Crowley. Though perhaps I could count on you to remain within shouting distance."

Crowley nodded his head. "I expect I can make myself available to you, should the need arise."

Crowley turned his horse away and started on a parallel course. The smile dropped from his face as he merged with the people moving about the bustling area.

---

Crowley knew that if you sit long enough, people tell the most amazing stories. It wasn't hard to find a place that was selling food, but finding one where the food wasn't dubious was more of a task. Still, Crowley managed well enough.

There was a tent not far from the first stable that had slices of roast beef, a thin gravy, and potatoes for a few pennies. A single penny bought a plate of beans from a pot that looked diseased. The establishment also had a bar, and that almost always guaranteed conversation. Crowley bought his food and settled in to listen.

Most of the people were talking of only two noteworthy things. The first was the silver in the area—amazing how many wanted it and how desperately they were willing to search for instant wealth. The other major topic of conversation was the ongoing Indian wars.

War might have seemed too harsh a word for some, but Crowley didn't think so. There were soldiers moving through the area, and they were there for the main purpose of pushing any red men they saw onto the reservations they had set aside.

Crowley had no idea why. Until a little over a year earlier he'd made a very strong point to stay well away from human beings in general, and while he was once again obligated to deal with people, he had no desire to get involved in their politics. One thing hadn't changed in his time on the planet: people got together and made messy political situations and then other people came along and tried to fix them. In the process there was normally a great deal of bloodshed. He didn't worry about politics. He worried about the things that tried to break into the world and take it for themselves.

A man standing a few feet away from him was speaking. The man was short, stout, and stank. He needed a bath far more than he needed a whiskey, but the drink was what he was after and what he was enjoying.

"Big as a bear," Stinky said, "and white as snow, and looking around like he's waiting to kill something."

Crowley could guess whom the man was speaking about.

The man pouring whiskey was taller, leaner and looked about as friendly as an executioner. Still, he nodded and poured and listened.

"Thing is, all the Indians is looking at him like he's gonna kill 'em and cook them up for dinner." The thickset man smacked his lips noisily and slurped down his whiskey like it was water. His mustache, desperately in need of a trimming, trembled as he spoke. "Far as I can see that would be an improvement."

Crowley kept his tongue. Ultimately, he didn't much see a need to involve himself in the discussion. Still it was interesting to hear.

When the bartender finally spoke it was softly, but with an edge. "Don't much care for the Indians, but I'm just fine keeping the army out of here, too."

"Oh to be sure," Stinky said. He had a sloppy smile on his face and he nodded his head so hard Crowley wondered how it managed to stay attached. "Any ways you look at this situation, I prefer to avoid having a hundred soldiers coming along and shooting the hell out of everything again. I already had that problem in Maryland, Virginia and in Alabama. I'm done with men in uniform."

Crowley snorted at that, not even trying to suppress the noise.

Stinky looked his way. His brow knitted. "You think soldiers are a good idea, mister?"

"No. I just don't think men in uniform will ever go away."

"How you figure?"

Crowley cut a piece of beef and chewed on it for a moment before answering. "You have silver mines here. People are staking claims and digging and some of them are making money. Those people are going to want to protect what is theirs, so they'll either hire men in uniforms to protect it, or they'll demand men in uniforms to protect it. Either way, you're going to get men in uniforms. Then you have your Indians, who maybe don't care about the silver and maybe do, but either way probably don't like getting pushed from place to place. They're going to get upset sooner or later and they're going to push back, and sure enough, more men in uniforms will come along to stop that from happening. I believe that's why you currently have men in uniforms heading in this direction."

Stinky looked at him for a long moment and then a smile broke on his face. He had a good smile. It made his face round and cheery. "Mister I like you. Let me buy you a drink."

"By all means," Crowley said. "But I'd ask you to do me the kindness of standing downwind. I'm still eating and you have a ripe odor on you."

Might be that some people would have taken offense to that, but Stinky did not. Instead, he laughed. "It's been a long few days riding to get here. Haven't found the baths yet."

The bartender pointed. "That way. Three doors down."

Crowley finished his meal and Stinky, who had forgotten all about the offer of a drink, went to get himself cleaned up. Really, that was better for everyone involved.

―――――――

Captain Henry Folsom looked around the settlement and glowered from under the brim of his Hardee hat. The men with him were tired and hungry and they needed supplies. He wasn't overly fond of the way the place looked, but they would simply have to work with what they had available.

There were Indians moving among the people in the camp and he didn't much care for that. His job was to make sure that the Apache stayed where they belonged and that was a task he took very seriously.

"Sergeant Barnes," Folsom spoke clearly, with a hard, barking note in his voice that perfectly matched his disposition. "Find stables and a spot upwind from this filth."

"Upwind, sir?" Barnes asked.

Barnes was one of those people Folsom always found offensive: they'd all been on the road just as long, but Barnes was neat and clean and not a hair was out of place.

"I have no desire to smell the people here if they reek as badly as the area looks."

Barnes snapped off a hard salute and broke away from the men.

When Folsom slid from his horse's saddle and landed, it was with remarkable agility. "Sergeant Fowler?"

"Yes, sir?"

"Take your squad and ride a circuit around this cesspool. I want to know how many Indians are here and why they are here."

"Yes, sir!"

A moment later the commander of the Seventh Battalion strutted toward one of the only solid structures he could find in the town. It was two stories of wood rot and sagging boards, but it was an actual building and that had to stand for something. The man who walked beside him was not Indian, yet he was not a proper white man, either. He said he was from China. All Folsom knew for certain was that Chi Chul Song was a better tracker than anyone else he'd met and that the fellow worked hard for a small wage. He did not speak to Song and the Chinaman returned the favor, but Folsom was happier with the man beside him than he was without him there. Song stood next to him with his muscular arms crossed over his broad chest and continued to say nothing while Folsom commandeered the Silver Springs Hotel for himself and his soldiers.

---

Lucas Slate felt the tugging at his body and soul like iron shavings might feel the pull from a magnet just exactly too far away to make them move. He could have resisted, but part of him did not want to. Part of him wanted this, needed to know what was behind the silent summons. What bothered him was he couldn't decide if that part was what he liked to think of as himself, or as the thing that was changing him. There had been a time when he could tell the difference with ease, but familiarity was not being kind to him.

What had once been a distant voice inside his soul was now a part of him, much as he hated the notion. The endless whispering influence that had already changed his body was now better positioned for chipping away at his mind. He still knew who he was, but recent events argued that he might not stay that way too much longer.

One nameless town, one odd beastie—odd enough that Crowley had never heard of it before—and the thing inside him had taken over, nearly drowning him in the dark waters of his mind. The change had happened so quickly that he couldn't fight it off. One moment he was himself, and the next something else had controlled his actions. It had worked out to the benefit of Slate and Crowley alike, but it had put a strain on their relationship, and though Crowley did his best to act as if nothing was different, Slate's mother hadn't raised any fools.

His horse clomped along as calmly as ever. The dogs in the area, and there were a goodly number of strays, barked and raged and backed away. The horse did not care. It wasn't really a horse anymore, of course. It had been snake bit a while back, when he and Crowley were in the middle of the badlands. The horse had reared up and run a hundred yards and then fallen on its side. By the time he'd reached the thing, it was dying. The muscles in its body were shuddering and the beast was soaked in sweat, surely as good as dead. Crowley had come along, moving at a leisurely pace. He'd stopped long enough to shoot the snake dead and then followed, but the look on his lean face said he knew what Slate knew: the horse was a goner.

And for only an instant, that dark whispering voice that seldom spoke loudly enough to be noticed on a conscious level had reached out and taken control. Slate had leaned down and grabbed the dying horse's head, wrenching it roughly around until the animal's open mouth was aimed at his face. He'd leaned down and exhaled a powerful breath into the horse's mouth and then held it closed with his hand.

He stayed that way until the animal shuddered and then shook him off. A minute, perhaps two, and the horse was up and fine and Crowley was looking at him with a calm that was even worse than the man's damnable smile.

Something needed to be done about what was happening inside Slate's body and his soul. He had no idea what that something might be, but he believed with every fiber of his being that the answers were somewhere near him, somewhere in this place. Just then he saw the palest man he had ever seen. Deathly white, actually. An Indian, that was obvious, but there was nothing natural about his hue or his demeanor. The man walked past him in the middle of a crowd, hunched over to the point where he looked easily a foot shorter than he should have. He had a shawl drawn over his head and if Slate hadn't felt that something was wrong, he'd likely have dismissed the shape as an old squaw.

The face that peered from under that shawl was drawn and ancient, thin and angular. The eyes were hidden in shadow, but he could feel them scrutinizing him just the same. The man stood up quickly and let the old cloth fall from his head and his shoulders, dropping it to the ground. Around them, most of the people paid no mind, but every Indian backed away as surely as if they'd been hit with boiling water and a few of them screamed, to boot.

When he smiled, it was worse than Crowley's. He spoke words that were not English. Slate should not have been able to understand them, but he did. The old man said, "I know you."

Slate shook his head. He spoke in English but knew the man understood every word. "I have never met you before. I'd remember you."

"You will know me better, soon."

It was at that moment that the Cavalry riders broke through the crowd. Slate had been so busy looking at the pale man that he'd lost track of everything else. The soldiers came on horses trained to bull their way through crowds. One of them had an old Indian woman by the wrist and was dragging her along beside him. Another had rope around the wrists of three younger women, also Indians, who were crying and trying to keep up with the rider and his horse.

Slate felt that other presence slither through his mind, but did not take the time to pay it any attention. He had other concerns. He was not fond of men who mishandled women. As a half-breed himself, he didn't much care what race they were.

He rode his horse four paces toward the first of the riders and allowed himself a very small grin of satisfaction when the horse reared up and threw the rider. The horse didn't like his mount. Most animals did not. As he rode forward a little more the rest of the horses grew skittish and backed up, despite their riders' urgings.

The first of the soldiers looked up from where he'd landed on his tail end and glowered up at Slate. Slate looked back down and kept his face deliberately expressionless.

"Watch where you're going, you damn fool!" The old woman backed into the crowd as the soldier stood up. Slate supposed he should have known the man's rank in the Cavalry, but he did not. He had never much cared for the soldiers he'd met and the feeling had always been mutual.

"I did nothing, sir, but continue on my way."

The man had risen to his feet and was still scowling, at least until he saw Slate's face a little better. As he shaved himself when he needed and looked at the changes in his features with a sick fascination, he knew what the man saw and that it was not particularly pretty.

"Well you've interfered in a military operation!"

"Wrangling squaws is a soldier's business these days?" Slate kept his voice as calm and soft as ever. Oh, he'd been riding with Crowley far too long. "I'd have thought you might actually try to find a few braves to fight instead of simply stealing their women."

"Get off of that horse, you bastard. You'll be coming with us."

Slate looked at him for a long moment and rested his hand on the grip of his rifle. "As I am neither a squaw nor a brave, I believe I will stay exactly where I am."

In the distance the other cavalrymen had managed to calm their horses—while successfully moving several feet back—and were watching what happened carefully. Apparently, the man who dragged old women around was in charge.

"That's a direct order!" He was furious, the soldier, but he was not very wise. He came toward Slate with one hand holding to his service revolver's butt.

Slate spoke softly; his expression remained calm. "I am not now, nor have I in the past, been a part of your army, sir. I do not answer to you."

"Are you a Confederate, boy? Is that the problem here?"

The man was likely a few years younger than he was. Not that it much mattered.

"In fact, sir, I was on the side of the North in the conflict, though I was not a soldier. I agreed with the notion that all men are created equal. I should think that would include red men, would it not?"

"What?" The soldier scowled and came closer still. Slate suspected he intended to sneak up and attack. He lacked in subtlety.

Slate sighed. "I am not a Confederate. The war is over, by the by. I am a gentleman. You might have run across a few in your journeys, though I fear it is just as likely you've never run across anything but gutter trash."

That seemed to be enough for the soldier. He stepped forward with every intention of pulling Slate off of his horse. His gloved hands grabbed at the reins of the horse and tried to lead it roughly away.

The horse did not move.

"You'd do well to leave my mount be, sir. He doesn't much like you."

"Piss on your goddamned horse!"

Slate sighed and climbed down from the saddle. The great grey beast looked at him with only the mildest interest.

Rather than bother with the horse he took hold of the cavalryman's ear and pulled savagely. The man screamed as cartilage snapped. While he was howling in pain, Slate punched him across the jaw and broke bones.

The next of the soldiers was already drawing his firearm.

Slate looked at the man and did the same. "Don't. It won't go well for you."

The man did.

It did not go well.

---

Stinky came back a while later. His actual name was Owen Napier, and he was a man without much purpose in his own estimation. "I come from a family of lawyers. They make a good living and I am fortunate enough to share in that, but I don't much like the law. Thought I might come this way and find something more interesting to do with my time."

"So you decided to try mining?" Crowley considered shaking his head at the notion because Owen-the-less-stinky didn't strike him as a very physical man.

"Lord, no!" Napier shook his head hard enough to rock his jowly face. "I figure if anything I might report on what happens here. Send articles back to a friend of mine in New York."

"Not a lot of money in that, is there?"

"I have a family. They'll keep me fed." He patted his belly. "As you can see that's not much of a consideration for me. Besides, they're glad to have me out here. I can't get in the way and I might have useful information for them, too." For a man who was carefully not admitting to being sent away from the family as an embarrassment, Napier seemed cheerful enough. When he patted his belly it also showed the bulge in his vest where he was smart enough to hide a small two-shot Wesson. It only took one bullet to kill a man if you were fast enough.

"So where are you from, Mister Crowley? I can't quite place your accent."

Crowley looked at his new acquaintance and smiled. "Here and there." Before Napier could ask any more questions, Crowley turned the tables. "What is it you have against Indians?"

"Hmm? Oh, nothing at all. But I keep hearing about raiding parties burning peoples' homes down and taking their women. That's a godless thing to do."

"Are you a scholarly man, Mister Napier?"

"I like to think so." He nodded. "Yes, I am."

"Look into your history a bit better and you'll find that raiding parties, houses being burned down, and women being taken from their families are not at all new notions. I don't believe there's a part of the world where it hasn't happened for as long as there have been people."

"Well, certainly not among civilized folks."

Crowley smiled again and Napier got a nervous look on his face. "Whatever makes you think a few buildings brings about a civilized human being?"

Before Napier could answer, Lucas Slate walked into the room, looming over everyone in the place. Most of the conversations died in an instant. Slate's voice remained as soft, and cold, and low as ever. Napier looked toward him and blanched. "Mister Crowley, I believe I'm going to need your assistance."

From outside the tent a slowly growing sound caught Crowley's attention. It was a noise he'd known for many, many years and one he never had much affection for: the sound of many men on horseback. Like as not, they were men in uniforms and their intentions would not be much to his liking.

"What have you gotten yourself into, Mister Slate?" Crowley did his level best not to smile, but it wasn't easy for him.

"There were a few men in uniform decided they had to take some ladies from this area without their agreeing to be taken. I intervened."

Outside there were the noises of commands being barked and repeated, horses coming to a halt and whinnying their displeasure, and a few dozen men working quickly to become organized in a chaotic situation. In other words, soldiers in action.

Crowley sighed and placed his hat on his head. "And did your intervention result in injury or worse to the men?"

"Indeed it did, sir."

"Well now, this should be something."

The man pouring whiskey looked uninterested. Napier seemed eager to hear more. He also studied Slate with wide eyes. He stopped when Slate turned quickly and stared back just as hard. Might be things would have gone wrong from there, but a collection of Cavalrymen came into the tent before things could get worse.

Of course, them coming in rather took care of worsening matters all by itself.

---

Folsom looked around. They were an unpleasant lot to be sure. The tent was filled with people, and most of them were unwashed and underfed. Folsom looked at the crowd and found the man his soldiers had reported with amazing ease. The gaunt albino was tall as he was thin and looked like death. He was dressed like a savage in rawhide, sported a coat made of some sort of animal fur, and carried two large pistols on his hips. Despite his uniform and the men behind him, Folsom hesitated for a moment. Then the Chinaman, Song, moved a bit to the side and a few more soldiers stepped into the tent beside them both.

Having an audience never failed to make Folsom feel the need to be brave. "You!" He stabbed a finger at the albino. "What in the name of God did you do to my men?"

The gaunt man looked at him. Next to him a smaller man with a feral smile looked in his direction with nearly feverish eyes. Most of the people were looking toward him, but what made those two different was simply that they were not afraid of him. Not in the least, and that was a worrisome thing.

The albino said, "I did nothing to your men that they did not provoke, sir." He had a southern accent. Little existed that was more contemptible in Folsom's eyes.

"I have four dead soldiers and a handful of men who swear you killed them. Attacking a soldier is a hanging offense." Folsom stepped forward and Song moved with him, a graceful, silent man with the eyes of a cat. Song always looked like he was ready to pounce, to kill, though Folsom had never once seen the man strike first.

"And I repeat, Mister Crowley, I do believe I'll need your help." The albino murmured to the smiling man next to him, seemingly unable to speak louder than a whisper.

The man with him slipped forward and stood between Folsom and his prize.

"Don't make this concern you, mister."

The stranger's smile grew broader and ice rimed the inside of Folsom's stomach. He had no idea why, but the man scared the hell out of him. Still, there were the troops to consider and justice to be handled.

"I know you. Henry Folsom. How's your mother? Ruth, I believe?" The man did not speak. He purred. Folsom felt that cold in his guts spread. His mother had passed when he was only ten. How the man could possibly know her was a mystery. Still, he seemed familiar,

"I do not believe we've met before."

"I know you. I know your father, Alexander. Your mother, Ruth. I knew your sister as well, Loretta." The lean man looked away for a moment, his eyes staring past Folsom toward something only he could see. Folsom barely remembered his older sister. She'd been involved with a man in Boston. There had been a scandal, of course, though his father did his best to hide it. Loretta died and died badly. The thought was enough to twist his heart into a knot.

"And your name?"

The stranger smiled. "I'm Jonathan Crowley."

Folsom backed up, his eyes growing wide. That was impossible, of course. He remembered Crowley. The man had seemed a giant to him when he was a child. He'd been tall and lean and he'd had the most terrifying smile.

"Good Lord." Folsom's lips barely moved. "How is that possible?"

Crowley's smiled dropped as fast as it had shown itself. He ignored the question and countered with, "I expect your men might have told you one version of the tale. Why not hear the other version before you decide how to handle the situation, Captain?"

The request was reasonable enough, but Folsom did not like the tone of voice any more than he liked that damnable smile. He didn't like the fear that seeing the man caused in him, either. "Your friend will have a chance to tell his side of the story when he stands trial." He wanted to dismiss Crowley, planned to, in fact, but the man stayed where he was and damned if that smile didn't come back and grow broader still.

Crowley's brown eyes regarded him for a moment and then he shrugged. "He won't be standing trial. He has things to do, and so do I." That was the end of the argument as far as Crowley was concerned. His tone said as much. Folsom looked closely at the man for the first time and shook his head. "Sir, you should take yourself away from this situation before it grows any worse. I have witnesses that say a man with skin as white as snow killed four of my men. I see exactly one man with skin as white as snow in this area, sir. In fact, I'd hazard there are no more albinos for a hundred miles in any direction."

"Would you indeed, sir?" The albino's face crept into a strange smile as he spoke. His eyes glittered under lids at half-mast.

"Have you seen yourself?" Folsom asked. "Your skin is as white as milk."

"Indeed it is. Has been my entire life. I did, however, have a conversation with another man not long before I saw your men, and he was just as pale as me."

The smiling man laughed and sent shivers down Folsom's spine. "Well now, I would hazard a guess you might be mistaken, Captain." His tone was dry and mocking and Folsom found him distasteful in the extreme. That damnable laugh, however, echoed in the back of his mind, brought back thoughts of his sister, and how he'd felt when he found her body.

No. The past was just that, and he'd not let the grinning fool confuse him with what had to be half-truths or blatant lies. How he knew about Folsom's family was irrelevant.

He had every intention of brushing the nonsensical claim aside, but before he could the man he'd observed pouring shots of whiskey spoke up. "Saw him myself. He's a little shorter, a lot thinner, and looks like he's an Indian, but his skin is just as pale."

"Nonsense." Folsom shook his head. "Corporal Bridges, kindly put that man in irons." He pointed toward the gaunt man.

Bridges nodded and took a step forward. The corporal was a burly man, large and heavyset, and capable with his hands. He'd knocked several men larger than him down a few sizes in his time and he would likely do so again.

The smiling man shook his head and blocked Bridges. "Let's not make a mistake here, gentlemen. My friend and I are perfectly willing to leave town right now and end this without any additional troubles."

"Are you deaf, sir?" Folsom's voice was as harsh as a whip crack when he spoke. "I have dead soldiers on my hands!"

"Your soldiers died trying to shoot me down." The gaunt man's voice remained as calm as ever, but the expression on his face belied his tone. "They were a mite bit offended, seeing as I stopped them from taking a few squaws to have their way with."

Was that guilt in Folsom's chest? He tried to tell himself that it was not, but he also remembered his sister, and the scandals she'd been involved in, and that feeling bloomed inside him. With an effort he crushed the emotion down. "It is our duty to curtail the growing Indian problems in this area. And in addition to confessing to killing my men, you've just confessed to interfering with that duty." He looked away from the gaunt man and barked at the corporal, "Bridges! Lock that man in irons!"

Bridges nodded and started forward. Before he could take two steps, the smiling man moved forward and struck him a solid blow that dropped the larger man to the ground.

"That's enough of this!" Folsom grabbed at the pistol strapped to his hip.

By the time he'd drawn, several of the soldiers with him were doing the same, and the two men he was facing had both managed to draw as well.

The smiling man had two Peacemakers. One of the large bore barrels was aimed at Folsom. The other was pointed at Song, who was crouching slightly and looked like he might well enjoy taking a bite out of the gunslinger.

The albino aimed a heavy shotgun at the whole lot of them. He'd swept the damned thing from under his coat with ease, and was looking hard at Folsom.

"Anyone pulling a trigger might well wish they'd reconsidered, gentlemen." A round-bellied man walked forward. His voice shook, but he had a pleasant enough smile on his round face. "Might I suggest we put weapons down and come to an understanding before anyone else is killed?"

Folsom didn't like him. He spoke like a lawyer. Still, he offered a chance to the captain not to get his head blown off by two different men. Outside of the tent several of his men let out bellows of anger and shock. The ground trembled lightly and while he feared taking his eyes off the two men aiming at him, he risked a look around to the entrance of the tent.

"Would someone kindly tell me what the hell is going on out there?"

Private Bronson called out loud and clear from the other side of the tent flap, "Captain! We got injuns coming our way! A lot of injuns!"

The smiling man laughed again. It was a humorless, bitter sound.

---

There was a point where no more could be tolerated. That point had come a long time ago as far as Alchesay was concerned. His parents had been murdered and scalped when he was a boy. His wife had been taken only a few years ago. His family had been attacked and slaughtered again and again over the years, first by Mexicans and now by the round eyes. Enough.

Several of the tribal elders wanted peace, but that time was past. They came into the area and looked for silver, and when they found it, they started digging. Most of the *Dilze'he* were already stuck in this desert land, forced here by the white man, and now they were being told to move again.

And maybe they would have. Maybe even Alchesay would have accepted this—though he was not truly sure if he would or not—but now these fools had come and dragged several women from the town. They thought the women did not understand their words, but they were wrong. His sister was among them and she'd heard what the men intended to do.

And according to her, a Skinwalker had saved them.

Whatever the case, it had only taken the word of his sister to send him toward the town, and because many of the men were just as tired of being pushed and pushed, they came with him.

There would be no more of their women raped or scalped by the white men.

The men in blue uniforms were gathered in one area when Alchesay charged into town with his men. In numbers they looked to be stronger, but they were all busy looking at one tent and before they were aware, Alchesay and his men were in range.

The first rifle shots cracked through the air before the soldiers did much more than look around with open mouths. All around the area people of all colors were running, wisely clearing away from the charging horsemen. Four of the bluecoats fell before any of them considered attacking in return. Two of their horses fell too, shot by who knew. Men and horses alike screamed.

And then the soldiers turned and grabbed for their weapons.

Alchesay had planned for this. Instead of staying at a long range, he and his men charged their horses into the enemy. Flesh fell before the hooves of his mount. Men screamed and fell, and the horse stumbled but kept its footing. He was too close to shoot, so he swung his rifle and hit whatever he could with the butt of the weapon. Someone fired from nearby and a bullet cut past his head. He had no time to consider that. Instead he hit another bluecoat and felt bone break.

There were screams, of course. And then there were battle cries. He called out for his men and they called out as well, and the cavalry recoiled as if hit by boiling water.

And he charged forward.

The tent was closer now. And the time was finally here. He would kill them all, every last one of the soldiers. They would all pay for what they had done, what they had planned to do. There would be no mercy.

Unfortunately, the men in the tent felt the same way.

There were more of the soldiers than he'd expected. They came from inside the large tent and started shooting and they were far enough away that they could still aim and shoot and kill.

Beside him Mangas stopped his battle cry when a bullet tore his skull away. He fell from his horse and into the tide of men being crushed, and that was the last Alchesay saw of his lifelong friend.

The bluecoats kept coming, and Alchesay jammed his heels into the horse's flanks and charged forward into the crush of soldiers.

And men screamed.

And men died.

And Alchesay roared his challenge for all of them. His skin felt hot. His bones were blades of ice. His heart thundered in his chest and his eyes shook in his skull.

And then the change came, and Alchesay roared his challenge a second time as his teeth grew and his body twisted into a new form.

---

Halfway across the camp he'd crouched in the dirt and made markings with one pale finger. His other hand had poured colored sand into the markings and filled them in.

The Navajo called his kind Skinwalkers. It was as good a name as any, but he knew better. There was more to them than just changing shapes. Most of his kind were gone now. They tended to kill each other off. It was not something they could, or wanted to, control. Like the weather or the stars, it was simply what was supposed to be. They felt a dislike for each other that could seldom be set aside for long. The one he'd seen earlier was a child, barely born into the world and likely knew nothing of himself.

He probably wanted to know more about what he was. And why he existed. The old one could have told him, but that was not what he planned this day.

What he planned was violence and carnage and blood and suffering, the things he fed on best.

And so he'd finished his simple spell and looked at the characters he had drawn in the dirt and then at the Apache charging into town. They had plans, too, and those plans were of blood and violence.

So the old one helped them along.

His hands had scooped up the colored sand and dirt and held the mixture out and blew it at the Apache as they rode past.

He did not hit all of them, but he'd hit enough.

He waited until they were engaged with their enemies and the bloodshed had begun before he said that words that made the spell awaken. And just that easily, the anger within the warriors was given a face and a form.

The old one settled down, and watched, and waited.

Soon enough he would feed.

Crowley shook his head as the cavalrymen turned away from him, and from Slate alike. Slate stared at them with an expression that was either shock, outrage or both. Whatever the case, it made Crowley chuckle.

"You find this situation amusing, Mister Crowley?" Slate looked his way with an expression of disappointment.

"Not at all, Mister Slate. I find you amusing."

"And why would that be?" Damned if Slate didn't sound offended.

"Because you look so very annoyed that the men who want to hang you are no longer bothering with you."

Slate blinked and a quick, embarrassed grin flashed on his face. "Yes, well, when you say it like that."

"We should leave."

"I agree." Slate pointed at the men flowing out of the tent. "But there are men in our way."

"This is a tent, Mister Slate. We can climb out from under it if we must."

The bartender looked at them and shook his head. "Could just go out the flap at the other side, too."

Crowley smiled and tossed the man a coin.

And as they were walking away from the soldiers, ignoring the screams and the gunshots, a deep roar shook through the air and the tone of the screams changed from anger and pain to deep, abiding terror.

And he knew before it happened of course. It was inevitable, really.

Someone out in the front of the tent let out a shriek and someone else called out, "Help me! Oh, Lord, help me!"

Crowley shook his head.

"You don't have to, you know." Slate's voice, as soft as a whisper.

"Oh, but I do." He shook his head again. "Can't you feel it? Whatever is out there, it's not natural." He spoke as if he regretted what was going to come next, but still the smile pulled at the edges of his lips and his heart beat faster in his chest.

"Well then, shall we do this?"

Crowley spun hard and nearly ran for the men at the opposite end of the tent. Many of the soldiers were coming back in, their eyes wide and frightened. He could understand that. There were a lot of things out in the world to be afraid of.

---

Folsom had planned to come out with guns blazing and eliminate the threat before it could become something larger. He'd half expected to run across a few of the savages in town, but when he heard the horses, and the sound of Apache battle cries, he felt a cold knot of dread in his stomach.

Had he, perhaps, turned a blind eye to his men having their way with the squaws? Yes. Why? Because happy soldiers performed better. What he had not truly considered was what might occur when the red skinned brutes found out about what was happening with their women. That was the very first concern when he heard the sounds of his men screaming. It shouldn't have been, but truth be told the guilt had been gnawing at him for a while.

The guilt went away the second he saw the monsters.

He'd pushed through the crowd of his men to assess the situation and was looking directly at the Indians when they changed. Not all of them, only a few, but it was enough. The man at the front of the charge was a stocky brute in leathers. He wore a canvas coat that had seen its best days a few years earlier and was coming apart at the seams, and his rage was a brutal thing to behold.

The coat tore itself apart, shredded right before the captain's eyes, and the clothes under it did the same, peeling away even as the man continued charging forward on his horse. One pace and the fabric was splitting. Another step forward and the horse was knocking two soldiers aside. A third step and one of the soldiers fell to the ground while the other kept his balance. A fourth step and Folsom was drawing his weapon, intent on killing the fool horseman. A fifth step and everything changed all at once. The horse let out a shriek and lost its balance falling forward and crashing to the ground. He was a horseman himself and knew instantly that the beast had broken its neck. The rider fell forward and *blurred* as he caught himself on his palms. That was the only way he could think of it. The fabric on his body was torn apart and so was the flesh beneath it. Folsom looked and his eyes refused to see properly. Great flakes of flesh and hair split away from the shape of the man and when he moved forward, standing instead of sliding across the ground, which seemed an impossibility by itself, he was not a man anymore but something entirely different.

The thing still had two legs and two arms, yet beyond that he would have been hard pressed to say what might seem humanoid about it. The body was wrong. Too broad, and covered in wiry fur. The head seemed to grow directly from the torso, and while he knew the thing must surely see, the only features that made any sense were the teeth that filled a mouth far too large for the rest of the hellish shape.

The thing roared again and Folsom aimed and fired, and then fired twice more. His aim was true, and a hole blossomed in the center of the demon's chest. It stepped back and then fell back and landed in the dirt, rolling and thrashing, slamming into the shuddering, dying horse, which once again let out a scream of panic and pain.

His men did their best to get away from both shapes, but even as they tried to escape the other horsemen were coming and they, too, changed. While Folsom was busy trying to kill the first nightmare a pack of equally-unsettling things dropped from their horses, snarling, bleating, screaming, and attacking the members of the Cavalry.

There were none of them the same. Each was a different form of nightmare; some thickset and low to the ground, others long-limbed and far too tall for human. The horses fled, kicking and screaming up a hellish noise, crushing everything that got in their way as they made as much distance as they could from the hellish things.

The only thing they had in common was that each and every one of the nightmares was, indeed, as white as the snow. They were ghostly, horrid things that scared him to the point he thought he'd piss himself.

The thing he'd shot got back up. It wasn't completely white anymore. There was a lot of blood spilling from the wounds he'd put in it, but that didn't seem to be enough to stop it. There was no face, just that damnable mouth full of fangs as it screeched and leapt at him.

And then the pale white man he'd been ready to lock in irons pushed past him and fired a shotgun blast into the open mouth of the thing. The barrel was just past Folsom's face and he felt the detonation as much as he heard it. After that he wasn't hearing much of anything. His ears were too stuffed with cotton to make sense of the words spoken.

Just the same, he understood the gesture when the albino swept him aside and fired the second barrel of his weapon. The thing he shot did not get up again. They were tough, but they were not indestructible.

Crowley was next, moving past him with no sign of a weapon in his hands and that mad grin of his spreading across his face.

His hearing was coming back enough that he heard the words from the smiling man's mouth. "What are they, Mister Slate?"

The gaunt man shook his head. "No idea, Mister Crowley, but I believe they are connected to whatever is drawing me here."

One of the things, too thin and too tall and reaching for a private who was screaming and staring down at the stump where his hand had been, turned its attention to the man named Slate and let out a sound like a cat hissing, if that cat was the size of a bear.

The man Slate had called Crowley stepped around the gaunt one and blocked the oversized hand that reached for the albino. He struck hard enough that the nearly skeletal thing reared back in shock. It was almost twice as tall as a man and had a face that was stretched and thin and filled with teeth the size of knives.

"No. I don't think you want to do that." Crowley kept smiling.

Folsom shook off his confusion and decided to handle the matter. The revolver kicked when he pulled the trigger and he watched the left half of the thing's neck explode in a gout of crimson that splashed both of the men.

Slate flinched as the thing screamed and clutched at the wound. That made Folsom feel a little better about his own fear.

Crowley stepped in closer and kicked the spindly leg of the thing with the heel of his boot. Bones snapped and the ghostly white demon fell as surely as if struck by an axe.

Folsom felt something touch his leg, and almost shrieked. He looked down and aimed his Colt at the source of whatever was touching him. It was Song. Half of the Chinaman's face had been carved into bloody red trenches and his eye was missing. He clutched at Folsom's pant leg and let out a sound. And then he died.

Folsom shook his head, angrier at the loss of the heathen than he would have ever expected. "That's enough of this madness!" he roared, and all around him the soldiers stopped their panic, or at least calmed it down. They were soldiers and they were used to combat. What they needed, what they always needed, was someone to lead them. "Kill these damned things!"

To make his point he aimed at the next of the things close enough for him to hit and fired. The shot went astray and only clipped one overly large ear on the beast. When it looked at him, really looked at him, Folsom knew he'd made a horrible mistake. He'd have apologized if he could have found the words, but it was on him far too quickly. Folsom let out a yelp as clawed fingers ripped into his coat and the beast lifted him into the air, baring impossible teeth and roaring directly into his face.

Folsom aimed his weapon and fired, and nothing at all happened.

He tried again.

Nothing.

"Well, damn." It was all he could think to say.

---

The captain was staring at his death, and Crowley was tempted to let it take him. As a boy he'd been a scared, confused little thing. As a man he smacked of too much cocky attitude and too little common sense. Worse, he was actually making himself useful. It was easier to ignore men who were useless and cocky about it.

Still, at the moment there were other considerations, like the damned things chewing their way through a dozen soldiers. They were monsters, yes, but nothing he'd ever seen before. They did not reek of the demons he was used to, and they were not spirits in any sense he was familiar with.

When he'd come to the New World, he'd done so to study these exact sorts of creatures. There had been a definite excitement in finding new and interesting beings in a land he had never been to before.

That excitement had not changed. Adding to it was the sheer variety of shapes that these creatures took. They were, he had no doubt, of similar ilk. They had to be.

Even things that ran in packs seldom liked to mingle with different creatures.

That was the part that made him smile.

Lucas Slate grabbed the thing holding the captain and hauled it backward by the scruff of its bullish neck. It let out a yowl of surprise and so did the Cavalryman. The good news for the captain was that it let go of him. That was also the bad news for Slate. The thing he was holding onto moved like a sack of cats held over a roaring fire. It twisted and whipped its arms in wide arcs and screeched as it turned on Crowley's companion, and both of them stumbled back and fell.

Before Crowley could get to them, they were lost in the crush of people.

A soldier aimed for the area where they'd fallen and Crowley knocked him aside, throwing off his aim as he waded into the crush of flesh. People moved and thrashed and pushed in and out of his view. Crowley ignored them all, save to push them aside. Somewhere ahead of him, not but a few feet to be sure, but in the press of struggling bodies it might well have been miles, his companion was down on the ground and fighting.

When the bullish thing flew through the air, it was as limp as a sack of horse dung. The thing trailed blood and as it rose into the air, Lucas Slate stood back up, covered in the same crimson stains and looking truly enraged.

His shirt had been torn apart and deep cuts ran along the left side of his muscular chest. Those cuts bled, a reminder that he was still at least partially human despite his appearance.

Slate looked around and stooped long enough to grab his fool hat from the ground. That hat had seen better days and likely would have been thrown away by most people, but the battered old thing with its dusty band and the broken feathers sticking from the same went back on Slate's head before he looked around and the rage faded from his expression.

It was a calmer expression he wore as he reached for his Navy revolvers and started aiming.

Crowley had the good sense to stay well away from the man as he pulled the triggers. The first bullet blew a hole through a white, scaly thing with too many eyes, and also took the hand from one of the Cavalry. The creature flopped to the ground and twitched. The soldier fell to his knees and screamed. By the time those two things had occurred, Slate had turned his attention to the next target and fired with that same dead expression on his face. *Boom!* The creature fell. Slate's mouth twisted into a feral snarl and he fired again. The bullets from his weapon were a reminder that death could be sudden and violent. Another explosive noise and the Indians and the soldiers alike were quickly backing away from Slate. He stood taller than any of them and he looked like the Grim Reaper ready for the harvest. The only things that didn't run were the white nightmares around them. They should have fled but it seemed beyond them to reason that well. Instead, they charged toward Slate and he fired again and again until the last of them fell at his feet.

Through it all, Jonathan Crowley watched with his eyes narrowed down to slits and a grin frozen in place.

When the final beast had fallen, Lucas Slate looked at Captain Folsom and shook his head. "I do not currently feel inclined to go with you for trial." Both of the weapons were still in his hands and the barrels of the Navy six-shooters were smoking in the cold air.

Folsom stared at the spectre before him for ten heartbeats without responding and then finally he said, "Currently, I do not feel much inclined to argue the matter, sir. We have all of us had a day already."

"Indeed."

Folsom called for his men to gather the dead and the wounded. His voice was weaker than before and his hands shook. That did not make him a coward in Crowley's eyes. It merely made him human.

He rather envied the soldier that.

---

Folsom sat in his newly-appropriated office in town. He thought about the day's events. All told, if you counted the Chinaman—and he did—he had lost seven men, and the number of wounded was higher still.

Somehow he had avoided getting injured himself. The men looked up to him and none of them had missed that he was in the heart of the combat. They knew he hadn't stood behind the lines and watched them take the damage. No, he had come out to the assistance of all when the damned Indians had attacked.

Being as he was in the middle of town when the attack took place he should have expected some sort of coalition of townsfolk, but he was caught flatfooted. The men who came before him were dressed, as gentlemen should dress, in proper suits with vests and with matching shoes. That was an accomplishment at least half the time; at least it had been since he crossed into areas across the Mississippi from home. That said, they needed a good wash and not a one of them seemed familiar with the idea of shaving their faces. The facial hairs were long and the facial expressions were dour.

They'd been droning on for a while now, long enough for him to get the gist. They wanted the soldiers gone. Or they wanted assurances, or they wanted the Indians dead. Something of that sort.

When he'd heard enough, he raised one hand and the conversations stopped. "What exactly do you gentlemen want? Pick one thing. I haven't the time to listen to every complaint you have. I need to report the deaths of my soldiers and I need to prepare your town for any more possible Indian attacks."

A black-haired man sporting the most impressive mustache Folsom had ever seen spoke, and as his lips moved, his mustache jittered and jumped. It was nearly mesmerizing. "There wouldn't be any Indian attacks if you'd left well enough alone." The man leaned forward and planted his hands on the long oak table the captain had commandeered to act as his desk. "We had us an understanding. We didn't piss on them and they didn't come along and try to kill us. You notice how they only went for soldiers? There was a reason for that."

Folsom stood up and gave the man his best hard look. It was a good one because the fellow took two paces back, shaking his head. "Do you know who I am, sir? Do you even begin to know why I am here? I'm here because I was called here by one of your own. A telegram was sent to

Washington, D.C. and that in turn was considered and then acted upon. I am the result of that telegram."

"And who the hell sent it?" The mustache trembled with righteous indignation. Folsom knew the man he was speaking to had eyes, but he had not yet been able to focus on them enough to consider the character they might reveal.

"Allucius Sheppard." Folsom reached into his jacket pocket and fumbled out the original paper. "Says here he's the mayor of this town."

The mustache tightened up for a moment and then trembled even more. "Al? Al Sheppard not only isn't the mayor of anything, he'd dead!" Several voices murmured their agreement. "The damned fool drank himself to death. Passed out and choked on his own regurgitation. And besides, he was never in charge of a damned thing around these parts."

Folsom felt a flush run into his cheeks. "Be that as it may, I have my orders to get rid of the red man in this area and I intend to follow those orders." He leaned onto the table and heard it creak threateningly under his weight. "I've spent time listening to your concerns, gentlemen. Until I hear otherwise, my duty is to remove the Indians from this area and keep your town safe. Good day."

"We were already safe!" Mustache shook his fist and looked like he might even consider using it against Folsom but decided at the last moment not to get himself shot. "Leave us to our own devices, sir! We have to live here when you're done with your damned orders."

The man turned his back and stomped away before Folsom could respond and after a brief hesitation the rest of the sorry lot followed suit.

Folsom settled back behind his newly acquired desk and started composing his explanation of the day's events. Colonel Hartshorn would want to know what had happened and he'd need to offer a proper defense. The loss of so many, and that on top of being caught unawares, was not going to sit well. Folsom dreaded the shit storm that would surely be coming his way.

He had no idea.

———

Lucas Slate looked in the dusty mirror and squinted at his reflection. The clothes were nice, a gift from Crowley, and they fitted properly. The tailor had a suit that was supposed to be picked up and never was—the man had died apparently—and while it took a bit of waiting while the adjustments were made, the final result was worth the patience.

Crowley eyed him critically enough to make him wonder if the man had ever spent time as a tailor himself. Finally he nodded his satisfaction, and counted out coins for the man who'd sold the suit.

"There is a haberdashery at the edge of the saloon over that way." The tailor pointed vaguely which, as the town had no proper streets, was the best that could be managed, "should you like a new hat as well."

Slate stared at the man for a moment and then simply shook his head.

Crowley walked for the door of the shop after thanking the tailor.

Slate watched Crowley break into one of his smiles. "What?" Slate was slipping his hat in place and almost managing a scowl.

"I have seen men less devoted to their wives than you are to your hat, Mister Slate."

"And had I a wife, perhaps I'd care less about my hat, sir."

"I should rather not consider the ramifications of that statement."

Slate reared back as if slapped and then chuckled. "You've a vile mind, Mister Crowley."

"Now, tell me about the pale thing you saw before everything went mad."

"He was tall and thin and pale. Looked to me as if he might be an Indian, but as washed of color as me." Slate looked away. "He spoke to me in some language I have never heard, but I understood him. He said we would meet again."

"You were pale when we met. You are an albino, after all, but you are a different sort of pale now."

"How do you mean?"

Your skin lacked pigment before. Now it has more color to it, but that color is white. That's really the best way I can put it."

Slate nodded his head and pursed his thin lips. "He was too thin."

"What do you mean?" Crowley looked puzzled.

"I mean I am thin, but I am still a possibility. He was taller than me and thinner than me. He looked impossible. His body is too thin and his arms and legs so very long and his head shape was thinner even than mine."

Crowley stared at him for a long moment and finally nodded his head. "That thing we dealt with in Carson's Point was a bit like that. But only a bit."

"I never truly saw the thing but towards the end, and frankly I was a bit too unsettled by what was happening to me to much care at that point."

"You touched a stone. The stone went into you. We've discussed that before, of course. We know that the stones were put into the—whatever the hell it might be's—chosen victims and they changed, but it wasn't the same as these things. These were sudden and the bodies didn't stay changed."

Slate looked at him. "Did they not?"

"No." Crowley looked back just as hard, his face impossible to read past that damnable grin of his. "They became what they once were when they died. They were Indians, but we knew that."

"Why do you suppose they attacked?"

Crowley shrugged. "I neither know nor care. Humans do stupid things to humans all the time, Mister Slate. I don't allow myself the luxury of paying much attention."

That was a lie and Slate knew it. They discussed many things on their travels and inevitably what they talked about most was the state of the world around them as gleaned from various newspapers. Crowley bought them and read them insatiably. Still, he did not call the man on his lie.

"And the soldiers? How do you feel about them being here, Mister Crowley?"

"I've never much taken to soldiers. Been one before, fought in my share of wars and followed orders, but I've never liked it. Soldiers are expected to follow orders, no matter how foolish those orders might be."

Crowley paused a moment and then asked, "And you? Do you side with the Indians?"

"No sir, I do not. I side with the people on the streets who are getting caught up in this conflict. I knew what those men intended when it came to the squaws." He shook his head. "I do not believe that women should be misused."

Crowley nodded his head.

"And you, Mister Crowley? Do you side with either group?"

"The Indians were minding their own business. The army was sent by someone. They do not, as a rule come without orders. They are summoned. So one is doing what they have always done and the other is following orders from elsewhere. I can't say as I much care either way."

"You keep saying that sort of thing, and yet, here you are, grinning and wading into conflicts."

Crowley's voice dripped with sarcasm. "My pale companion has gotten himself into trouble and asked for my help. What is man to do?" His plain face looked around the shop for a moment and then back to Slate. "How does the suit feel?"

"Like proper clothing, and I thank you for it, Mister Crowley." Slate ducked his head briefly for a moment, feeling an unaccustomed flash of shame. "I fear I cannot possibly pay you back any time soon."

Crowley waved it aside. "I have the money to spare and you have lost all you owned before we met. As we are traveling together for the present time, I can hardly expect you to settle into life as an undertaker again, though I imagine you could have made fair compensation this particular day."

"Just the same."

"Should I decide you owe me, Mister Slate, you may rest assured you'll be informed of such debts. Until then, merely accept that under our current circumstances I do not mind investing in your clothes." He snorted. "Besides which, you were beginning to look too much like an Indian and I need to not confuse you for any other white-skinned Indians we might encounter."

"Do you suppose that's a strong likelihood?"

"You've run across one already and I am fairly certain you are looking forward to a second encounter."

"What makes you say that, Mister Crowley?"

"Because you have a need to understand your place in the universe, Mister Slate."

"And you don't?"

"I have known my place in the universe for a very long time, Mister Slate. And we are still looking into your position."

Neither spoke of what might happen when that position was known.

———

Finding rooms proved challenging, but not impossible. Apparently having a giant albino looming over your shoulder made people more willing to find space for a man in a negotiating mood. The rooms were comfortable enough, and as an added bonus seemed bug free.

In the morning, Crowley looked at the growth on his face, and trimmed the hairs down to manageable levels rather than shaving them away completely. He knew it wouldn't last, but for the next few days at least he had a neatly-trimmed beard and mustache to fight off the cold.

When he came downstairs, Slate was already waiting for him, and the small gathering of tables were all filled except for the one where the albino waited. His hat had been mended and looked mostly like it had in the past. Crowley chose not to feed into his obsession and ignored the thing completely. Within twenty minutes they'd eaten and after ten minutes more they were on their way.

"Where are we going, exactly?" Crowley asked, though he already knew the answer.

"I'm off to find the other one like me. You are along to keep me out of trouble."

Crowley nodded. "I seem to remember something about that."

"As it was your idea, I should hope so, sir."

Despite the violence of the day before, the crowds were moving about, many of them looking to buy wares and others looking to sell. It was distinctly possible that there were even more wretches moving into the town.

There were soldiers everywhere they looked, though for the moment none of them seemed to be causing too much trouble. Crowley had no doubt that would change soon enough.

Folsom had made clear that he intended to clean the Indians from the area for the safety of all involved, regardless of how the people felt about that. As it had been Indians starting the shooting the day before— excluding what Slate had accomplished all by himself—it seemed perfectly reasonable to expect the captain and his men to be as prepared as possible.

A pickpocket tried to steal from Crowley. He stopped the attempt without causing a scene. It was a bad time to be a thief and a worse time to be a child. He decided to let someone else deal with handing the young boy with the grabby hands. The things they'd been bothered by the day before were far more worrisome. Besides which, Crowley kept most of his money hidden where it would never be found. A moment later he changed his mind, and contemplated going after the kid and teaching him a lesson, but it was too late. The would-be thief was long gone.

---

He watched the other Skinwalker from a distance, and noted the man who walked with him. They were both powerful, as was expected of any Skinwalker, but the one with him, the smiling man, he was a different sort of powerful. He carried himself with confidence and he smiled at almost everything. Not a pleasant smile but a baring of teeth, a warning that the man was deadly beyond most people's reckoning. Where they walked, people scattered away from them, perhaps without even being aware of it.

The Skinwalker was aware, of course. That was why he was following them. They were dangerous and they could well be dangerous enough to cause him harm. He would find out soon enough.

The wind blew and whispered its secrets and he listened as he had learned to long ago. The stories of the wind were all about the Indians coming toward the town. There had been a great deal of blood spilled and the Apache in the area wanted to settle the matter. They did not wish to talk any longer. There is a point where anyone can lose hope of a simple resolution and that time had come and passed.

All around him people moved and milled and sought desperately for what would make their lives complete. An urchin moved toward him, furtive and worried. He bumped into a man in front of the Skinwalker and plucked a few coins from his victim's pocket. A moment later he was bumping into a young woman and apologizing even as he lifted a small item from her bag. And then he bumped into the Skinwalker, mumbled an apology and continued on with a small silver nugget the Skinwalker had been carrying for the last three days.

The silver meant nothing to him. He had taken it from a dead man he found on his way to the town. The corpse had been torn open by what at first glance appeared to be wolves, but the Skinwalker knew better. He could smell shapeshifters and found the notion amusing.

The fact that the boy took it merely meant that he had managed to catch the old sorcerer's attention. That was enough.

A whispered word as he crouched and grabbed at the soil. The arid earth crumbled in his hand and he spat into it, rubbed it between his fingers and his palm until it became a doughy mass. He stood just long enough to throw that simple lump at the thief, striking him on the back of his neck. The boy reached reflexively for what hit him and the old man smiled and continued on his way. Only a few seconds later the screams started as the boy fell to the ground, swelling and choking and trying to breathe. It was not the first time he'd spread a sickness and it would not be the last. This was a minor one and would only kill a few, but it would leave them all afraid.

Somewhere behind him a woman screamed as the boy's flesh rotted away and spilled his bodily fluids into the street. Up ahead, far enough along that they did not seem to notice, the other Skinwalker and the strange creature walked on.

---

Crowley noticed Slate cock his head to the left. "What is it?" he asked.

"That damn song again," Slate replied. "Every time I hear it something goes wrong."

"You are hearing a summoning spell. Whatever this thing we're looking for is, it summons energies and what I can only call demons, even if they don't feel like the ones I'm used to."

"Then how do you know?"

"I've been testing your limits, Mister Slate. Seeing what it is you might be capable of, but I have my own abilities."

"You've never much discussed what they are."

Crowley cast a sideways look in Slate's direction. "We don't much talk about what happens if I decide you are a threat. We both know the answer already, yes?"

"Of course." Slate nodded his head, but his voice remained soft and dry. "I might be a threat and you might need to eliminate that threat. We've already seen a little of what something like me can do. If I don't maintain control, I understand what you'll have to do and I condone it."

"Do you?"

Slate looked at him and his mouth trembled for a moment. "I've no desire to become the sort of monster I was raised around."

"You were raised around monsters?"

"I was raised an albino and a mulatto in an area where many considered that a sign of the Devil, sir. Had my family not had a certain level of influence I'd have been killed. As it was, I remained locked inside my house most times to avoid a beating. There are all sorts of monsters, Mister Crowley. Not all of them cast spells or have fangs."

Crowley nodded his head. "Agreed. Very well, Mister Slate. A few facts for you. I can see the dead. I can communicate with them. Mostly I choose not to."

"Why is that?"

"Because the dead are not of interest to me. They are dead, and often they make demands when they know they can be heard. I am not interested in their demands and I have no desire to be plagued by them anymore than I have been in the past." Crowley's face grew troubled for a moment.

"Are the dead around here?"

"Some. Not as many. Not too many have died here yet, though I imagine that's to change soon."

"Are there any dead around us now?"

"Oh, yes." He looked past Slate's shoulder at the faint ghostly image of Molly Finnegan and nodded slowly. She looked at him, implored him, would have begged if there was enough of her left, but there was not. Something had stolen most of her away in Carson's Point, not too long ago, and left just enough to ensure he was haunted by her. He had not yet resolved to destroying that remnant or sending it on to whatever lay beyond this realm. If he didn't think about it, he could tell himself she wasn't suffering. Sometimes, most times, really, he didn't much like himself. He promised himself that he would release her soon. Very soon. Just not yet.

"What else to you see that you do not speak of, Mister Crowley?"

"I see a lot. I hear just as much. I heard the spell that was cast. I'm still trying to understand it. I know that it came from behind us, but so do you."

Slate nodded his head. "I do indeed. I've been trying to decide how to handle it."

"Well, perhaps you should confront your enemy and be done with it."

"Is he my enemy?" Slate's voice carried an uncertain note.

Crowley stopped walking and stared hard at him. "I should imagine he is. He's killed several people with his actions, and a few moments ago he killed a young boy who was seeking enough to stay alive in this hellhole."

"Did he?" Slate shook his head. "How do you know that?"

"Because currently the dead boy is standing over his rotten remains and screaming his rage into the skies. You cannot hear the dead, Mister Slate, but I can and I do."

Slate closed his eyes and nodded. "Then I suspect he is, indeed, my enemy."

Crowley heard the sound of gunfire and screaming from the far side of the small town, same as they had the day before. The screams were not pain or suffering. They were war cries. "Well, things are likely to get confusing right about now." Crowley spat the words, but again his smile crept out.

"I suspect you are right, Mister Crowley. And should I confront my enemy or wait?"

"It might be that the fighting won't reach us."

Slate nodded again and spun hard on his heel, moving back the way they'd come.

Crowley watched him, watched the crowd that had turned toward the sounds of dying part before Slate as easily as calm waters part before a ship's prow, and watched also as the small shape he approached unfolded itself from a stooped position.

Lucas Slate was taller now than most of the men around him. He was taller than Crowley by a few inches, though they had only recently stood almost the same height. Crowley had once stolen a suit of the man's because it fit well enough to allow it. As tall as Slate was, the thing that stood before him was taller by almost a foot. How it had hidden itself in so small a form was a mystery that Crowley would try to solve later.

The thing was the same color as Slate, a white that seemed too vibrant for the cadaverous shape. It had long white hair tied back in a braid, and wore clothes that looked like rawhide but that Crowley knew immediately were human flesh.

It had a very long body and a long face, eyes as dark and black as pitch and as shiny as polished glass. When the nightmare smiled his gums were gray and his teeth an unpleasant shade of yellow.

Slate and the thing spoke to each other, and Crowley listened and understood not a word of it. In the distance a dead boy kept screaming his outrage about being murdered and further away still, the gunfire continued in sporadic bursts.

---

The Indians came in hard and fast, and this time there were more of them and they were better organized.

Folsom's men were doing their duty, guarding the town, and none of them took their task lightly. The day before had been reminder enough that their work was dangerous.

So when the red men came, the alarm was quickly called. Folsom stepped outside and prepared himself for the battle. The men were ready and so was he and by God, he'd see the savages pay for their bloody assault.

The men rallied quickly and he called for them to assume the various posts around the small town that he'd laid out the night before. They were ready and they were more than willing after seeing their companions taken down. One or two might well have been worried about whatever sort of monsters the Apache had brought with them the day before, but they rallied just the same and he was proud of them.

Captain Folsom walked away from the hotel and headed for the sounds of conflict, his heart pounding with the thrill of combat. He was not afraid. The Lord had blessed him with a brave heart and a noble purpose. He would see the day through and take no prisoners. The savages had earned a quick death for their troubles.

Up ahead of him, Sergeant Barnes had taken a position on top of a two-story mercantile, firing as quickly as he could into the crowd below. The man was hell with a rifle, and with each shot, an Indian dropped, but damned if it didn't seem there were endless numbers of them this time around.

He had dealt with the Lakota before but never with the Apache until the previous day. They did not seem cut from the same cloth. They seemed more determined to stand their ground and take whatever it was they wanted.

"Fowler! Where is Sergeant Fowler?"

"Sergeant Fowler is on the other side of town, standing his ground and waiting, sir!" The man that spoke to him was just out of his sight, but he recognized the voice of Private Herbst. The voice was as distinct as the man himself, a red-haired brute nearly as strong as an ox. He turned to bark an order at Herbst and saw the private's body jerk twice, saw the blast of meat and bone that came off his left shoulder and then saw the man hit the ground, screaming.

Damned foolish of him to look away from the conflict. He looked back toward the crush of Indians coming into town and the chaos of people getting away from them. The civilians ran, as well they should. The soldiers stood their ground.

Folsom drew his revolver and took aim at the closest savage, a lean old man on a black horse. The old man saw him and charged, riding hard to reach him. The bullet he fired caught the old man in his thigh and blew through the leg and the horse under it with ease. The old man screamed, the horse screamed, and both collapsed in a sliding heap. Neither was dead, but he intended to remedy that. One step closer, and the bullet from the next Indian caught Folsom in the chest, tearing through the rib above his heart and then through the organ itself. He tried to aim his weapon but his traitorous fingers dropped it. The pain, when it showed up, was as large as a mountain and crushed his chest in its grip. Folsom tried to scream, tried to do anything at all, and managed only to fall backward and land hard on the ground. The horse and rider stomped over his body as they continued into the town, followed by several other natives.

---

Crowley watched on from a distance, his face calm and almost expressionless, his eyes intensely focused. Slate did his best to ignore the man, which, considering the nightmare in front of him, was not that difficult.

"You have questions," The thing said. It was a statement rather than a question. Again it was spoken in a language other than English, one completely unknown to Slate, but he understood just the same.

"What are you? What am I?"

Those vile teeth flashed and the impossibly thin, tall man chuckled. "You were given a seed. It was planted in your body. I do not see it." It stared for a moment and then pointed to the small bump almost perfectly centered in its own forehead. When he touched it the skin parted like an eye blinking and for just an instant a greenish-gray stone showed before the skin sealed itself again. "It would be similar this, but not exactly the same."

Slate remembered touching the stone and feeling it, remembered that pebble, too, had a song to sing. He nodded but did not speak.

"That seed is what you are. What you are becoming. We are not many, there have never been many, but we are powerful."

"What do I do about it?" Slate asked.

"Embrace the changes. I fought mine and in the end it caused me nothing but pain."

"What is the song I hear?"

"That is magic trying to tell you how to grow and become strong."

"Do you hear that same song?"

The thin man looked at him with a cold, sly expression. "I am the song."

"I don't understand."

"We are a part of the world. This world and others. We can listen to the song and we can sing notes from the song and create wonders. But we must feed if we listen to the song."

He wasn't sure if the thing was being deliberately vague or simply lacked the ability to explain himself. Either way, he was starting to dislike the thin man.

"What do we have to feed on?"

"Mostly pain, and others like ourselves." That smile grew larger.

Then the thin man reached for him and placed a hand on his chest and something inside of him pulled and twisted and shook through his body like a tree's roots being ripped from the ground. Lucas Slate tried to step back, tried to break free, but the thin man's hand on his chest burned at him and left him unable to move a single muscle. He stared at the yellowed teeth in darkened gums surrounded by white, smiling lips, and felt hatred rip into his heart.

In a lifetime full of predatory people who thought he was easy prey, Lucas Slate had proven more than his share of people mistaken. He could not make his body move. He could not make his anger known by any of his previous methods. He could not, by God, even call out to Jonathan

Crowley a dozen strides away. Instead he listened to the song that called to him and tried to understand the things it was saying.

The pain fought for his attention. The song had been trying to get his notice for longer.

He let the song win.

---

Crowley stared hard at the two pale men, waiting as they stood face to face and spoke. He could not understand a single word they were speaking and that, too, was something he was unaccustomed to. He did not understand because the words were new to him, but they were also not words, not exactly. Damned if it didn't sound like two of them were harmonizing.

As a counterpoint to their song, the battle raged close by and coming closer. The Cavalry was fighting against the invading Apache and by the sounds of screams, cries, and gunshots, the conflict was in a full fury.

Crowley stared toward the direction they'd come from and saw the soliders retreating, heading at a slow crawl toward where he stood and watched another war taking place.

Sometimes the conflicts seemed impossible to escape.

Then the gaunt man facing off against Lucas Slate slapped Crowley's companion in the chest and Slate started jittering where he was, standing still and twitching, seizing again and again. The usually calm face pulled down, drawing into a pained expression and Slate's eyes raged silently.

Crowley'd planned on doing nothing at all about this. He made it habit not to get involved in several different sorts of situations, not the least of which were cases when one monster fought another.

Did he think Slate was a monster? That was the question.

Not far away the dead boy kept screaming his anger to the skies. He refused to be placated by whatever it was the afterlife was supposed to offer him. From the corner of his eye he could see the vaporous spectre of Molly Finnegan, dead since the previous winter, buried by none other than Lucas Slate and whose body once pushed itself out of the ground at the behest of whatever sort of creature Slate was becoming.

Behind Molly a Cavalryman's head snapped back violently and he flopped to the ground without making a sound that could be heard from the distance. Molly looked at the body expectantly. Crowley looked away.

Helping Slate would be a hideous mistake. The events of the last summer had proved that beyond a doubt. The man had muttered words and shattered the ground at his feet. He was no longer human.

And yet, as Slate asked for help in the tent earlier, Crowley was still allowed to respond now. He was freed from his usual constraints when asked for assistance by a human being.

And he was freed when asked by Lucas Slate.

"Damn me," he muttered.

The gun was in his hand in a second. He cocked the hammer, aimed and fired. Aimed, fired. Aimed, fired, and then again.

All four bullets slammed into the thin man. The first shot surprised him. He had apparently forgotten Crowley was there. The bullet tore his right arm apart, dragging it from Slate's chest. Slate staggered backward, gasping. The second bullet took the thin man in the left shoulder blade and spun him where he stood so that he was looking toward Crowley's feet. The third round punched into the thin man's chest and blew a hole through his left lung. The fourth round hit him in the stomach and doubled him over as sure as if he'd been kicked by a horse.

The thin man gasped and grunted and then fell to his knees, trying to balance himself on his hands. He bled from each wound and Crowley could see the streams of blood flowing to the ground. Crowley took three strides forward and looked down at Slate where he lay on the frozen soil. Slate looked at him and sat up, wincing. Where the thin man had touched him his shirt was torn and the skin underneath was already bruising, showing an amount of red that would have been alarming on most people, but for all Crowley knew that the color was perfectly normal in an albino who got himself bruised properly.

"I wasn't sure if you were going to help me or not." Slate's voice was raspier than usual.

Crowley did not answer the statement. To his left he saw the thin man standing up.

"Mister Crowley!" Slate's eyes grew wide, and Crowley looked at the pale shape rising and immediately stood. The thin man was looking hard at him and he was scowling. His face, already long and thin, grew longer still as he opened his mouth to speak. What he said meant nothing at all to Crowley. It was just gibberish. Just the same he felt his body hurled backward and did his best to prepare himself for impact.

The good news was that he landed on a canvas surface. The bad news was that a cast iron stove was under that canvas. He felt his ribs break on impact, and his right arm snapped in three places. He did not black out. He was not that fortunate.

---

The Skinwalker looked at his prey and smiled again. The wounds hurt, but he would heal. He would take from the younger, weaker Skinwalker and he would feed on the essence as had been done for as long as there had been Skinwalkers. Each was born, each created their seeds, each offered the seeds to worthy humans and then left. Later, after the seeds had a chance to grow, they came back and harvested their children. This one was not one of his, but that did not matter. He would feed and he would feed well and if the one who created this one took offense, he would feed on the progenitor as well.

The young Skinwalker stood up and shivered. His chest was an angry red mass. The bruising was no doubt painful. The seed was deep inside this one's chest, near his heart. That was why he'd grabbed him there. Most Skinwalker's chose to place the seeds in the forehead. It made it easier for their children to see with their new senses and it also made harvesting them easier.

"I will kill you now. If you stay still, I will try to make your death simple." It was a mercy he was willing to offer.

The young one nodded his head and said, "Fuck yourself." The shotgun rose and both barrels of the weapons fired at him.

The Skinwalker had been alive for a very long time and he was familiar with European weapons. Familiarity, however, did not prepare him for the pain. A hundred tiny pellets rammed through his flesh and burned into muscles, into bone. One of the tiny shots tore open his right eye and the agony was greater than he had felt in lifetimes.

He yowled and fell back, clutching at his face. He had planned to be merciful. That plan was finished.

He looked through his good eye in time to see the young one breach the shotgun and pull out the hot shells. As he watched two more were inserted and the gaunt man came closer, scowling down at him.

He raised one arm and sang. His right arm was ruined and hadn't had time to mend, but his left worked well enough. His fingers clenched the air and he pulled with his song, with his mind, willing the seed deep in the other to come to him, to tear free of its moorings and come to him.

---

Lucas Slate dropped the shotgun and clutched at his chest. Was this a heart attack? He had no idea, had never felt one before. The pain grew larger and he fell to his knees, crying out.

Had any pain ever been this large? His hands held tight to the front of his chest, and under the palm that touched his pallid skin he felt something moving, twisting. He remembered the day he'd swallowed the oddly carved pebble he'd been given as a gift. It was a memory he'd done his best to forget, a fevered dream he never wanted to recall.

Much like the pain tearing him in half.

Lucas Slate screamed, something he hadn't done since his transformation had started. The sound was not remotely human.

---

For three seconds Crowley had a fantasy about Molly. Her body was next to his and she whispered in his ear, a warm breath that tickled pleasantly. Then the pain kicked in and took him from his reverie.

There was magic about and while he often hated that notion, Jonathan Crowley was healed by the presence of the supernatural. His skin ached and his bones shrieked a symphony of pain, then the agony faded into a deep fiery itch as they pulled themselves where they belonged and healed within him.

Crowley opened his eyes and stared at Slate and the thin man. Both of them were on their knees, straining and bleeding and locked in some sort of silent struggle. Slate did not seem to be winning. He would rather Molly whispering in his ear, but she was dead and the past offered him little solace.

"All right then," he moaned. It was only a moment for him to stand up.

The sounds of gunfire continued and grew closer, drowning out the cries of the dead pickpocket and the unsettling scream coming from Slate.

Crowley started walking, heading for the two of them.

The first of the Indians came into view and almost immediately reined in their horses. They stared at the thin man and Lucas Slate with expressions of dread that were nearly comical, and grew almost as pale as the two of them.

He had no idea why the Apache were so afraid of the pale men and he did not care. What mattered at that moment was that the whole marauding lot of them watched for all of five seconds, and then their leader let out a command that had then turning tail and leaving the area at high speed.

As Crowley had witnessed, the Indians in the town had been scared of Lucas Slate. Apparently two of his kind in the area was a bit too much for them to stand. Crowley smiled at the notion, even as he looked back to Slate and the thin man.

Slate screamed again and blood spilled from between the fingers clamped over his chest. His eyes were wide and his mouth moved like a trout out of water seeking a gasp of proper breath.

"Move your hands, Mister Slate!" Crowley bellowed the words and the thin man ignored him.

Slate looked at him and managed a puzzled expression. "I am...I can't. What do you need?"

"I need to see what he's reaching for inside of you."

Slate stared at him for a moment and slowly, carefully let his hands fall away. The lump that was revealed was the size of an apple. That Slate's chest had not exploded was something of a miracle in Crowley's opinion. Heavy lines of red stained a great deal of his body and in addition to the heavy lump trying to tear free of him, there were other lines, other things moving under his skin. All of them seemed connected and all seemed determined to come out.

Crowley looked away from Slate for only a moment to assess the thin man. He'd been beat down a good bit. Four holes from the bullets Crowley himself fired and more still from a shotgun blast or two. Only one eye remained and it stared only at Slate.

The bastard was smiling.

Crowley hated when other people had a reason to smile. Well, at least when they were enemies of his. He walked closer, scrutinizing the thin man's face.

One eye was gone. One remained. Centered above them was a small opening in his head, and that at least was something Crowley was familiar with.

He had seen similar stones in Carson's Point. They had caused him no end of troubles.

Two fast steps had him picking up his pistol. Three more strides and the barrel was one inch from the center of the thin man's forehead.

As he cocked the hammer back the bastard finally noticed him and his one remaining eye opened wide. Crowley pulled the trigger and ripped the top of the thin man's head away with one shot.

The thin man launched backward and slammed his ruined head into the frozen ground. Deep within his skull a collection of grey things wriggled. They all seemed to be seeking something that was no longer there.

Crowley looked at the body for a moment and then checked the remaining portion of the skull. The bullet had managed to destroy that damned stone, whatever it might be, and though he couldn't be sure, he suspected that was a mighty fine thing, indeed.

Slate fell forward and caught himself on his hands again, whimpering.

The sounds of combat were gone. The noise of people screaming had died as well, though in the distance a dead boy wept with less fervor, perhaps one step closer to accepting his fate.

Crowley put his weapon away and helped Lucas Slate to his feet.

"Are you well, Mister Slate?"

"I am not, sir. But I am alive and I thank you for that." His voice was fainter than usual.

"You'll have to be well enough." Crowley squinted as he looked around. "You take the Indians and I'll handle the soldiers."

"What do you mean?"

"I intend to stop this damned fighting before one or both of us is killed."

Lucas Slate nodded his head and rose to his feet. He hefted his shotgun and looked toward the direction the Indians had gone, to the direction of most of the fighting.

As he walked, he murmured under his breath, words to a song that no one else in the vicinity could hear or understand. The furious red marks on his torso rapidly faded, first to pink and then to the same color as the rest of his flesh.

He was learning. The song had many, many notes and Slate suspected he would not know them all for years, but for now he learned how to heal himself with the song and it was a start.

---

Crowley found Sergeant Fowler and his men gathered near the far side of town, following orders. They were there to make sure the Indians didn't come in from the other side of the area, and likely to clear a path should it become necessary to flee Silver Springs.

Crowley walked directly up to the sergeant while the man watched warily.

"Sergeant?"

The man nodded and came toward him with caution. There was no telling where a man might stand on the Indians. Most agreed they should be sent away, but wise soldiers didn't take that for granted.

The spell was simple, and one of the very first he'd learned ages ago. Crowley didn't like using sorcery on human beings, but if he had to, he made exceptions.

"Sergeant I'm sorry to inform you that your captain and most of the rest of your soldiers are dead. They were killed by the Indians, who are fleeing even as we speak. You've won the battle, but the cost was high."

There was truth to his words, but only as much as he needed. He could have told the man that it was the heart of summer and he'd have agreed. That was how sorcery worked.

"I'm sure they fought bravely." The sergeant's voice was slightly slurred.

"Of course they did. They fought valiantly and they won. But wouldn't it be best if you returned to your base camp and reported in? If more Indians should come back they might see your presence as a challenge and you can't do your duty if you're all dead."

The sergeant looked around uncertainly. There were seven men with him. The rest were elsewhere or dead.

"Yes, of course. We'll head for home."

"An excellent idea, sergeant. You have to make sure your men are safe, after all."

He finished the incantation. The sergeant would forget having seen his face. The men around him would remember only that the sergeant had been informed of their pyrrhic victory and nothing else.

A short walk had him reuniting with Slate and with the man who stood near him. Stinky Napier was clean and sober, his eyes haunted by the sights that Crowley didn't need to see to understand. There were dead men up ahead and likely a lot of them by the sounds from earlier

Not but twenty feet away Stinky was staring at the two of them with wide eyes. Crowley smiled broadly for him. Napier flinched a bit but stood his ground.

"And is the town still alive, Mister Napier? Or are we the only survivors?"

"Oh, there are more, Mister Crowley. The Indians only wanted the soldiers. They were good about not shooting anyone else." He frowned a moment. "Can't say the same for all the soldiers. Some of those boys shot anything that moved."

"Still think the red men are all heathens?"

"Absolutely. Doesn't mean I have to hate them. I just know they do not properly worship Jesus Christ."

Crowley shook his head and said nothing. That was a story he was wise enough not to touch on.

"What happened to the Indians, Mister Crowley?" Napier's voice caught him off guard.

"They saw my friend and the other pale man fighting and ran as fast as they could. I have no idea why."

"Can't be that many soldiers left." Napier's frown deepened and he looked around. "I don't reckon that's a bad thing just now."

Slate spoke up, his voice still pained. "Might we be on our way, Mister Crowley? I'm feeling a bit faint."

Mister Napier opened his mouth to say something else, but one look from Slate silenced him.

------------

When the morning came, the two men claimed their horses from the stables. A surprising number of the Cavalry's horses were gone, despite the lack of riders, but no one was foolish enough to try for theirs.

"Where are we headed today, Mister Crowley?"

Crowley looked at his companion and shrugged. The weather was hideous, but that was hardly unusual. "I took the time to listen to a few men chatting last night, after you had gone to sleep. The men were French and talking about *Loup Garou*."

Slate frowned. "Werewolves?"

"You speak French, Mister Slate?"

"Not as well as I speak English, but I can manage. Spent a bit of time in Louisiana and dealt with my fair share of Cajuns."

Crowley nodded. "We're heading west, Mister Slate. We shall discuss what happened here when you feel more inclined to discussing the matters, but we are heading west to see if there are, in fact, werewolves hiding somewhere in the region."

"You don't suppose it's merely wolves?"

"No. In my experience, wolves very rarely attack wagon trains."

Slate nodded. "Well then, I imagine this will be an interesting journey." The man seemed distracted and Crowley simply nodded. Let him have his time to think.

------------

As they rode, Lucas Slate listened to the song that always played for him and, in listening, began to comprehend.

# What Rough Beast

by James A. Moore and Charles R. Rutledge

Deputy Tom Morton stood at the edge of town, staring into the dark gray, snow filled sky. The noon stage was now six hours late. The snow was getting heavier and night was coming on.

"Tom," a voice said from behind him. "Come back in the saloon, son. Watching the road won't bring the stage in any faster."

Tom turned to face Deke Potter, owner of the general store and an old friend. Tom said, "I know, Deke. But Hanna is on that stage. Don't mind saying I'm getting pretty worried."

Deke gave a quick nod. "You standing out here getting frozen ain't going to help her none. Come inside and maybe we can get some men to go out and see if the stage has had trouble."

Tom followed, but he didn't have much hope of putting together any sort of rescue party. Most of the able-bodied men in Cider Creek had gone with Sheriff Adams two days before, in a posse hunting a group of men who had robbed the local bank and killed three people. The rest were afraid to go out after dark because of a rash of apparent wolf attacks.

Stepping inside the saloon didn't raise Tom's hopes any. Most remaining town folk were home by now, bringing livestock in, and hunkering down for what looked to be a severe storm. The majority of the men left in the saloon were too old or too drunk to go riding into the snow. Still, he had to try.

"Excuse me, boys," Tom said. "As you men know, the stage should have been in a good while before now. With the sheriff gone, I need a few men to ride with me and see if the stage has floundered in the snow or broken a wheel or something."

Most of the patrons didn't look his way and the few that did quickly went back to staring at their drinks or their cards. Tom felt himself flush with anger. Didn't these men know that his wife was on that stage? He was just about to say something to that effect when someone spoke from the saloon's far corner.

"I'll go with you," a deep voice rumbled.

Tom looked toward the speaker. He hadn't noticed the stranger when he had come in. Though the man was seated, Tom could tell that he was a big one. His shoulders and chest were massive and his hands, one of which almost swallowed a whiskey glass, were huge.

"I'm obliged, friend," Tom said. "I don't think we've met. I'm Tom Morton."

The man said, "Kharrn."

Kharrn rose from his table and for a moment Tom didn't think the man would ever quit standing up. He was close to seven feet tall if he was an inch, with skin almost as dark as an Indian. Hair like an Indian too, but no Indian ever had those cold blue eyes.

Tom said, "Anyone else?" No one spoke. "Looks like it's me and you, Mr. Kharrn."

"Just Kharrn."

"Whatever you say, hoss. How soon can you be ready to ride?"

"I'll go the livery stable and get my horse now."

Deke said, "I'll go too, Tom. I ain't so old that I can't ride with you. You and the big fella come over to my store and I'll get us lanterns and blankets and what have you."

"I'm obliged, Deke."

Deke shook his head. "If it wasn't for your Hanna, I likely wouldn't have survived the influenza last winter." He glared around the room. "And that's true of more than me."

The front doors swung inwards and two more men entered the room. Tom looked at them and felt his skin crawl a bit. The shorter of the two, the one who was just average in height, looked normal enough. He had brown hair, brown eyes and a long, lean face. His expression was as dour as one might expect from someone coming out of the bitter cold of the storm.

The other one, however, was a different story. Tom had seen his share of death over the years, from when he found his father dying from a rattlesnake bite, to dealing with a few of the soldiers that managed to get themselves killed in the war between the states, and not a one of them looked quite as ghastly as the apparition ducking under the lintel of the doorway.

He was almost as tall as Kharrn, but much thinner. He wore a good suit under a heavy bearskin coat, and sported a battered and much abused top hat adorned with a scattering of very misused feathers. His attire was not the issue, however, it was his face, a gaunt, nearly withered affair with thin lips, a long chin and nose and half-lidded eyes that were a very faint blue. The color of his eyes was bold in comparison to the stark, dead white of his flesh. White snow melted in white hair that ran down to the shoulders of his jacket. The deputy had never in his life seen an albino, though he had heard of them a few times.

"Crowley?" Kharrn said.

The brown-haired man shook the snow of his gambler's hat and stared at Kharrn for a moment before his face broke into a smile that promised pain and suffering and foul intent. Despite the extremely dark grin he walked forward and shook the larger man's hand.

"Do you ever plan of dying, Kharrn?"

The bigger man's hand nearly swallowed his and he craned his head to look up at the first volunteer to come to Tom's aid.

"I could ask the same," Kharrn's voice rumbled, deep and low.

The voice of the other man, the pale one, was just as low, but soft and close to a whisper. "I sometimes wonder if there is a place on the Earth where you do not know someone, Mister Crowley." A southern man, to be sure, but there was nothing about him that said he was ever a member of the Confederate Army. He looked toward Kharrn and nodded his head. "Mister Crowley has spoken of you, sir. He did not exaggerate your size."

"The deputy was asking my help. There's a stagecoach lost in the storm and his wife is among the passengers." Kharrn stared at Crowley for a moment before continuing. "Would you help if asked?"

Crowley's grin faded a moment and then flashed again. "Are you asking?"

"It's a harsh storm and I suspect you didn't come here to get out of the weather. Yes, I'm asking." There were meanings hidden in the words. Tom did not know what the subtle context might be and he did not much care if he could find more people to help.

"I'm asking as well. My Hanna is out in that storm and several hours behind schedule. Will you help us? Will you help me?"

Crowley broke his eye contact with the giant in front of him and looked at Tom for the first time. His smile was gone but damned if he didn't seem amused. "Of course. Mister Slate will help as well, won't you?"

The gaunt man spoke, stepping closer and making the deputy's skin want to slither away and hide. He did not answer Crowley's question, but instead looked directly at the deputy, his eyes remaining half-hooded even as they studied his face. "Which direction are they coming from? We've been riding from the east and every sign of a road is missing. The snow is up past my knees out there."

"From the north. They should be riding next to the river."

Crowley made a low noise.

Slate nodded his head and looked around the room and the gathering of men who were not coming with them. His expression did not change. "Let us hope the river is visible. It's getting dark out there."

Kharrn, who had been staring at the man called Slate with a curious expression on his face, spoke up. "Then we should be on the way. The night won't get any brighter."

Accompanied by Deke and this strange trio of allies, Tom stepped out into the snow. A hard wind came sweeping down the main street, burrowing at Tom's clothes and driving crystals of snow into his exposed skin. He hated to think of Hanna stranded out in this weather, but he did his best to push those thoughts down and out of the way. Right now he needed to focus on finding the stage.

The three strangers retrieved their horses and met Tom and Deke at the store, where bundles of blankets and supplies were distributed amongst the riders. Tom eyed the horse under Slate with the same sort of dubious caution. The beast was enormous and didn't seem to breathe enough to make a mist come from its muzzle whenever it exhaled into the cold air. Without further conversation the men mounted up and together they rode into the gathering twilight.

Tom noticed that Deke kept as far away from the strangers as possible, especially the pale man in the stovepipe hat. Not that Tom blamed him. There was something disconcerting about the albino. Not just his looks either. Slate seemed to radiate a kind of…wrongness. Then again, Tom would have ridden side by side with old Satan himself if it meant finding Hanna.

"How long has it been?" Crowley called to Kharrn over the wind. "That dust up with Dickens in London?"

Kharrn nodded. "That seems right. Took me two days to dig myself out of those tunnels. What happened to you? I thought you might be dead."

"Thought the same about you. I was swept down the underground river into the Thames."

Tom had no idea what the two men were talking about. They seemed to have some history though. Another gust of wind swept across him and for a moment Tom thought he heard it howling, but then he realized that the sound wasn't the wind.

"Did you hear that, Mister Slate?" Crowley said.

"I did indeed," said Slate.

"Wolves," said Tom. "There have been attacks on some of the outlying ranches in the last few weeks." He hoped that bit of information wouldn't send the men scurrying back to town.

"Heard about that," said Kharrn. The big man looked over at Crowley and Crowley gave him a quick nod.

"I heard it might not be wolves. Not exactly." Crowley almost grinned as he spoke, and Tom felt a flash of unease and suppressed it. Hanna was what mattered.

"I can just make out the river through the snow," Tom said, pointing to his left. "We should be able to follow the river road by keeping the water in sight."

The riders steered their horses down toward the dark strip of river. The water looked black in the fading light. Daylight was almost gone and the snow continued to pile up.

"Should we light the lanterns?" Deke said.

Crowley said, "Not until we have to. Make us too easy to see."

"Well that's what we want, ain't it?" said Deke. "If the stage is broke down out here, maybe they'll see the light."

"And maybe something else will too," said Crowley.

"Let's push on as far as we can without the lanterns," said Kharrn.

Deke frowned but he didn't argue. Tom heard another wolf howl and the sound seemed to be picked up by a second animal and then a third.

The howling gave Tom a chill deeper than the storm. Still, he had never heard of wolves attacking a party of men, and the group was certainly well armed.

It seemed to Tom that the snow was falling heavier as they rode. It was like moving through a white fog that obscured all details and muffled all sound. Tom started as he thought he caught something move out of the corner of his eye. When he turned his head in that direction though, there was nothing.

"Ever see a pack of wolves kill an elk?" A quiet voice said from right beside him. Tom jerked his head around to find the cadaverous Mister Slate riding close by.

"It's not like you'd think," Slate continued. "The pack doesn't all run in and tear the elk apart. That's dime novel drivel. No, one of the wolves will run up and nip at the elk's legs. Try to hamstring him. Then the pack will back off and wait. After a while they'll run in again and try for another bite or two. Get him bleeding good. Pretty soon the elk can't run or fight. Then the wolves will get down to business."

Whatever reply Tom would have made was interrupted by Deke Potter's screaming. Tom wheeled toward the sound. Deke's horse was down and Deke was hanging loose in the grasp of something out of a nightmare.

The thing was tall and lean and covered with bristling gray fur. It was roughly man shaped but its face was that of a wolf. Its muzzle was covered in blood and flesh that it had ripped from Deke's throat. As Tom watched, two more figures appeared out of the snow to crouch behind the first. Their eyes glowed yellow as they glared at Tom.

"Oh Jesus," Tom said, "Oh Lord." He clawed for his Colt and pulled it free of the holster, firing even as he raised the weapon. One of the wolf-things began to stalk toward him, growling low in its throat. Tom emptied the Colt into the gray horror, but the creature didn't even slow down.

"Bullet's won't stop it, lad," Kharrn said, stepping up beside Tom. Tom glanced at the big man and saw that Kharrn held an enormous ax with two blades.

The wolf-thing growled again and lunged forward. It was fast, oh so fast, but Kharrn sidestepped and swung the big ax. The creature leaned away and the ax missed, leaving Kharrn off balance for a moment. The wolf-thing swept forward, claws spread to rend, but Kharrn twisted and swung the ax in a back handed stroke, catching the monster in the torso, ripping open its abdomen and sending blood and entrails steaming into the snow.

Tom staggered back and fell to the ground, his heart hammering. What the hell were those things and where had they come from? And Deke! Deke was dead.

Another of the things charged toward Crowley, dropping to all fours and coming in low, likely preparing to gut his horse with claws and teeth. Rather than drawing a pistol the man threw something that struck the monster in the eye and sent it falling back, yelping in agony. It flopped back into the snow and both of its unsettling humanoid hands covered the upper part of its face. Below those hands the teeth of the beast gnashed and snapped together as if to tear the pain to pieces.

The third creature circled around Crowley on his horse, also low to the ground and rumbling deep in its chest. As it moved, Lucas Slate climbed down from his great gray horse and reached for his shotgun.

The advancing demon charged for Crowley, leaping over its wounded brethren before bounding forward. Crowley's smile was as broad as the monster's.

Before it could reach him, Slate fired a blast from his shotgun into the monster's side. It let out a surprisingly high-pitched yelp and fell sideways, but got up immediately. Crouching, favoring its wounded side the wolf-beast locked eyes with Slate and came for him, teeth bared and a warbling sort of half-roar coming from its chest.

As it charged Slate met it full on, a glint of metal held in both fists.

He managed to duck the claws that tried for his face, but they tore into his bearskin coat and pealed it down his chest in shreds. He fell forward, grunting, but caught himself against the monster's side.

Claws flashed and so did the knives in Slate's hands. The coat was torn apart but it had served its purpose when it came to protecting the man.

Tom looked for a chance to assist him, but there was too much going on, too much to see. Crowley had dropped from his horse. The nightmare facing him was wounded. One eye was gone and a thick trail of gore dribbled down its face, but it was still coming, still murderously enraged.

Kharrn had finished his dark work, but the thing he'd killed still didn't want to stay dead. Parts of it steamed and moved. The deputy looked at his useless weapon again and cursed under his breath.

Slate let out a hoarse gasp and stepped back from his enemy. The body lay in the snow and bled. The ghastly white stranger looked around in the darkness and the sight of him made the cold only a secondary reason for Tom's chill. The coat he'd worn was torn away but the man called Slate hardly seemed to notice. He loomed over the dead thing and shook trails of blood from both of his weapons.

"How are you cutting that damned thing when my bullets did nothing?" The words were out before Tom gave much consideration.

Crowley stepped out of way as the wounded beast came for him again. So far he seemed gifted at not getting hit.

This time, as the creature lunged past, he drove his hand into the bleeding wound in the monster's head and it crashed into the snow and stopped moving. "Kharrn? Would you kindly take the head from this thing?"

The big man obliged with a hard sweep of his oversized blade.

The horses did not look at all happy with the current situation and Tom had to struggle to keep his roan from bolting. Deke's horse was screaming, a sound that sent razors through the deputy's nerves.

Slate was moving toward the downed animal already.

Crowley nodded his thanks to Kharrn. "Werewolves."

"What kind?" Kharrn's question threw Tom as much as the declaration. He'd heard occasional stories of shapeshifters from a few of the locals who traded with the Apache, but he'd never given them much credence until now.

"See for yourself." Crowley reached down and pulled a weathered old wolf's hide from the shoulders of the beheaded corpse at his feet. Beneath that hide was the body of a naked man in his middling years.

The body beneath was lean, and the skin was pale.

"Not an Indian," said Kharrn.

Deke's horse stopped screaming. The sudden silence was almost worse.

Slate started back their way and stopped after only a few feet. "I think I see the stage up ahead. It doesn't look good."

Tom squinted into the snow, trying to see what Slate meant. He couldn't make out anything through the dark and the storm. The pale man must have had good eyes.

Crowley looked toward Slate and where he was pointing. "I guess we should finish this then. Let's see what we can find out."

"Hanna!" Tom called, running past the other three men. After going several yards in the direction Slate had indicated he saw a shape, darker than the night, looming ahead. It was the stagecoach all right, but there was no sign of horses or of any living thing.

In his haste to reach the stage Tom didn't see the area of dark, partially melted snow until he slipped in it. There was a great quantity of fresh blood on the snow not far from the stage's side door. Heart pounding, Tom regained his feet and staggered to the stage. He found the door handle and jerked the panel open. In the darkness he could just make out two figures, but he couldn't see them clearly. Please God, he thought. Please let it be her.

"Tom?" Hanna's voice said. "Oh Lord, Tom. Is it really you?"

Then she was in his arms and for a moment the terror of the last few minutes lifted. "It's me Hanna. It's sure to God me."

"Tom, we have to get out of here. There are…things out there. Things that ate the others."

"I know, sweetheart. I know. I've seen them."

"And you'll see more of them before the night is through, deputy," Crowley said.

Tom turned toward him. "You mean the three you killed weren't all of them?"

Crowley gave a short bark of a laugh. "Not hardly. It's a pack of shapeshifters. The snow's covering their signs fast but from the tracks there are several more. How many you think, Kharrn?"

"At least five more," the big man said.

"You were always a good tracker," said Crowley.

Five? They had barely survived an attack by three of the monsters. How could they hope to get Hanna back to safety with five or more of the things on their trail? They were down to four horses and the snow was getting deeper by the minute.

"Excuse me, deputy," a new voice said. Tom looked back at the stage and saw a small, wiry man in wire rimmed spectacles peering out of the door. "I'm Henry Parker. You men seem to know about these devils from hell. What are they?"

"They're not devils," said Slate. "I've seen devils. These creatures are shapeshifters. Werewolves. We thought they might be Apache Skinwalkers, but apparently not."

Parker's eyes grew very wide as he looked at Slate. Tom didn't blame him. The pale man had managed to arrange what was left of his coat as best he could but a large amount of white skin still showed through. Incongruously, his stove pipe hat still sat at a rakish angle.

Crowley said, "What happened, Mrs. Morton?"

Hanna looked toward Crowley and Tom felt her shudder in his arms. Hanna said, "Those things overtook us about a mile back. They could run as fast as the horses and they...they seemed to enjoy chasing us."

"Wolves love a hunt," said Kharrn.

Hanna nodded. "After a while they leaped onto the horses and brought them down. Then they tore them apart and ate them. Oh God, Tom. We have to get out of here." She buried her face against Tom's shirt.

Crowley said, "You tell us what happened next, Parker."

Parker made a swallowing noise in his throat. "The driver and his man shot at the devils but it didn't bother them one bit."

"Told you they weren't devils," Slate said.

"Yes. Sorry. The werewolves then. They attacked the driver and the other man. Then..." Parker trailed off.

"What?" said Crowley.

Parker swallowed again. "There were four other passengers in the coach. They dragged them out one by one and ate them alive. I think they enjoyed making us watch."

Kharrn said, "Shows they're still part human. Real wolves don't kill for fun. Just to eat."

"Then they heard us coming and sent three of their number after us," said Crowley.

"So where are the others?" said Tom.

A chorus of howling started then and Crowley gave one of his sardonic smiles. "All around us, deputy. We're surrounded."

"You came here looking for these things, didn't you?" said Tom, remembering some of the things the three men had said.

Kharrn said, "Came looking for something. Wasn't sure what, exactly."

"While we had a little better idea, didn't we Mister Slate?"

"We did. Though we had hoped to find whatever it was under less unfortunate circumstances, Mister Crowley." said Slate.

Tom said, "What can we do? Put Hanna on a horse and send her toward town while we hold the werewolves here?"

"She wouldn't get a hundred yards before they ran her down," Crowley said.

Kharrn said, "Put your woman on a horse anyway. We'll have to try and walk the horses out of here. They can't run now. Snow's too deep."

"We can't wait any longer," Slate said. "The shapeshifters are closing in."

"How do you know?" said Tom.

Slate smiled. "I know."

Slate came up to him and captured his hand long enough to place the hilt of one of his daggers across his palm. Tom stared for a moment before remembering how little good his pistol had done. He nodded his gratitude and found himself wondering why the man wasn't shivering violently in the cold. The wounds on the man's chest had looked worse before. They were little more than scratches despite how they'd bled earlier.

Kharrn said. "The woman goes in the center. Ring the other horses around her. We'll have to fight a running battle."

"What about me?" Parker said.

"You take your chances with the rest of us," said Kharrn. "Now let's move. Slate is right. I can feel the werewolves close around us."

They arranged the horses as Kharrn had said, with Tom leading Hanna's horse. Tom would have given anything to have his wife far, far away, but there was nothing for it. He knew one thing. If any of the other townspeople had come along, they'd be dead now. That made him think of Deke. What would he tell Deke's daughter Abigail? He pushed the thoughts away. All that mattered now was keeping Hanna alive.

"So you were looking for some sort of supernatural creatures out here, Kharrn?" Crowley said.

"I heard rumors. You know what I do and why I do it."

"Still haven't worked off that debt yet, eh?"

"Don't know that I ever will."

"But you had your revenge."

"Oh yes."

"And was it worth it?"

The big man grinned a savage grin. "Oh yes."

Crowley nodded his head. "I took a little time off. Didn't work the way I'd hoped. Found Slate here on my way through California. Still haven't decided what to do about him.

"I can hear you, Mister Crowley." The albino's words were as soft a whisper as ever, but the tone was petulant.

"I know that." Crowley's smile was a slash in the darkness. He did not sound contrite, merely amused.

One of the horses gave a shriek of pure terror and Tom saw the animal stumble as two of the werewolves landed on its back, biting and tearing. Kharrn leaped to where the horse had fallen, swinging the ax over his head and down. One of the blades took the closest werewolf in middle of the forehead, splitting its skull. Blood, bone, and brain splattered across the big man's face. Before Kharrn could turn to the second werewolf, the monster was on him and the two went down, struggling.

Tom heard a blast from a shotgun and spun. Three more of the werewolves were rushing toward Crowley and Slate. Nothing he could do there so he turned back toward Kharrn. The giant man and the werewolf were rolling over and over in the snow. Blood was splattered everywhere and Tom saw that Kharrn's coat and shirt had been shredded. The werewolf's claws were doing horrible damage to his upper torso.

Tom heard Kharrn cursing, and then the big man was on his feet and he had the werewolf's head grasped in his huge hands. The creature was still ripping and tearing at Kharrn's flesh but Kharrn gave a quick, hard twist to the werewolf's head and Tom heard the thing's neck break from where he stood. With a growl that almost matched that of the shapeshifters, Kharrn twisted the head again, actually pulling it clear of the monster's body and casting it aside. He stalked forward and snatched up his ax from where it had fallen. Kharrn was bleeding from a dozen deep gashes, but his eyes seemed to burn with a frightening vitality as he looked around for another foe.

Tom stood next to Hanna, easing her behind him. He'd die before he let anything happen to her. His hand reached for his gun without thinking and only the remembered weight of the hunting knife stopped him. The blade gleamed in the faint light.

Slate fired the shotgun again, the blast catching one of the beasts. It flopped backward, the force of the shot knocking it sprawling, but it yelped as it fell and he knew it was still alive.

As he watched, one of the beasts leaped at Crowley. The man moved to the side and grabbed the werewolf as it passed him, his fingers catching the thick fur and sinking into the pelt. The creature tried to turn away but he held on, fighting the thing, holding it with a strength that belied his size.

The third of the beasts charged directly for Tom and Hanna. Tom did not think. There was no time for thinking. Instead he moved his hand up and drove the blade into the monster's underbelly. The edge was keen and cut into the monster as if through water. Forward momentum rammed the hilt deep into the belly and then up, into the heart of the werewolf. Its oddly shaped legs collapsed and it staggered.

For one instant Tom thought it was over. Then the thing roared and lurched forward, teeth snapping and eyes rolling madly. It had blue eyes, human eyes. The face was all wolf except for those damnable eyes. Hanna let out a low gasp behind him and Tom felt the blade try to slip from his grasp and hot blood stained his hand to the wrist and tainted the color of his coat.

Who knows what a man can do until the time comes? Tom let out a roar of his own and caught the hilt in a double-handed grip, rather than let it escape him. He pushed against the dying thing and wrenched his hands upward, the knife continuing its trek until the throat of the beast was cut all the way to the jaw. The werewolf flopped to the ground, its insides steaming in the cold.

Hanna let out another noise and Tom stared down, watched as the body began to change and the fur pealed slowly away like the rind from a drying fruit.

"Tom? What's that?" Hanna's shaking hand pointed to a glimmer of black metal that rested in the snow. How she even spotted it he couldn't begin to guess. The piece was small and a severed leather cord ran through an eyelet at the top of the design. He didn't want to see it. The amulet hurt his eyes and his head.

Not quite daring to touch the piece, Tom leaned down and poked it with the tip of the silver blade and then jumped back as the obscenity let out a hiss as surely as a heated horseshoe dropped in cold water.

Whatever the design was, it withered and blackened as the blade touched it. Tom thought of a spider caught aflame as he watched.

Crowley said something to the werewolf he was holding onto. The thing was moving around and trying to break free but the man had a grip on it and wouldn't let go. He'd seen men thrown from horses that put up less of a fight. Crowley was hurled one direction and then another as the thing tried to force him away but he still clung tightly.

The werewolf let out a howl that ripped through the night and lunged. At first he thought the beast was charging toward him and Hanna, but at the last moment it changed coarse heading for Parker. The man didn't seem at all surprised.

He seemed worried, but not in the way Tom would have expected.

Parker reached out for the werewolf and touched the beast's arm, his fingers clutching at the fur.

"Bethany!" The word was out of his mouth and only then did the man seem shocked. He pulled his hand back and shook his head, even as Crowley drove the werewolf's head into the snow at his feet.

"I'll kill her, Parker!" Damned if the man wasn't smiling as he spoke. The werewolf was still thrashing, still fighting desperately to get away, but Crowley's hands had the beast's arms pinned and he crouched over the struggling beast showing impossible strength.

"No! Not her! Damn your eyes, don't you hurt her!"

Crowley leaned down and hissed words into the werewolf's snow-drenched ear and the beast shrieked, a sound even worse than the death cries of Deke's wounded horse.

A moment later Crowley pulled back, tearing the rippling, thrashing fur from the screaming shape.

Where the wolf-thing had been a naked woman now lay, whimpering in pain, her lovely face a mask of agony. Her bare skin steamed in the cold night air.

Crowley hurled the writhing fur into the snow after hissing more sounds into it, sounds that were as unsettling as the necklace had been.

Motion from the corner of his eye made Tom look away for an instant. Slate was walking toward them, his pale chest painted crimson. A deep scowl marred his already unpleasant face.

There was no sign of Kharrn, a man who was nearly as tall as a tree. He couldn't imagine the man running away.

The furs that Crowley had thrown aside smoldered in the darkness and then flared with a silvery light. The thick pelt caught fire, burning and still moving, as if still somehow alive.

Henry Parker stared bloody murder at Jonathan Crowley and spat a stream of venomous, obscenities into the air between them. Tom had no idea what the words meant, but again felt revulsion at their tones.

Crowley staggered back and waved his arms but whatever he was trying to do failed. He was thrown through the air and ricocheted off a tree before falling into the snow. The darkness had taken most of the night but the burning, screaming furs—screaming! Would the madness never end?—gave off enough light to let him see the blood around Crowley's fallen form.

Parker snarled. It was not a sound a man could make. Tom looked on as the man grew. He expanded, and his clothes shredded themselves, falling away.

"All I wanted was a family! A pack of my own! A man needs a family! A wolf needs a pack!" His voice warbled and changed as his flesh fell away, revealed the creature underneath. This was a werewolf, to be sure, but so much larger than the others. Different in other ways, too. Tom could feel the raging menace coming from the black furred nightmare that looked at each of them with murderous eyes.

"I'll see all of you dead, except for you." A thick-clawed finger pointed at Hanna. "You'll be the first of my new pack."

Tom felt that he was as close to the edge of madness as he'd ever come. He was a churchgoing man and the good book said that there were creatures of evil loose in the world, but he had never thought to see anything like this. But whatever that thing was, it had threatened Hanna. No! Worse. It had threatened to make her a creature of darkness like itself. Tom hefted the silver blade.

"I won't let you touch her," Tom said. "Go back to hell where you belong."

The thing that had been Parker laughed and the sound was chilling, coming from a throat that was not designed for human laughter. "You truly think you can stop me, little rabbit? You're all prey to me. I've enjoyed the game, even when I was pretending to be one of you, but that's over."

The werewolf began to stalk forward, huge shoulders hunched, fangs glittering yellow against the fast-falling snow. A low, rumbling growl came from the creature's throat and it leaped for Tom with outstretched claws.

Slate's shotgun boomed again and a big chunk was blown out of the werewolf's thigh. The thing howled and twisted toward Slate. The pale man cast the empty gun aside and went low under the raking claws that swept out. Slate had his knife in a backhanded grip and he used it to cut a deep gash across the werewolf's ribs.

Parker returned the favor, dragging his claws upward across Slate's torso and tearing two deep cuts into the albino's chin. Slate's head snapped back with the force of the blow and he went rolling across the snow. Parker rushed in, spittle flying from his jaws as he snarled in rage.

A dark and massive form came hurtling out of the snow to land between Parker and Slate. With a cry that was half growl itself, Kharrn lunged, cutting with his ax. The blade sank deep into Parker's belly, and the werewolf howled as it staggered backwards.

But Kharrn wasn't letting the creature get away. He moved in, swinging the ax again as if felling a tree and this time the heavy, two-bladed weapon struck with such force that the werewolf's spine was severed and before Tom's disbelieving eyes, the upper half of the monster fell away from the lower half.

Ropes of entrails went spinning away and blood spattered everywhere, covering Kharrn and marking the snow with a pattern only some dark god could read. Blue eyes blazing, Kharrn continued to hack at the body of the fallen beast until it was nothing but a red ruin. Finally, he backed away and stood to his full height, holding the ax over his head and bellowing into the night.

Hanna, who had crept close to Tom whispered in his ear. "Mr. Kharrn isn't turning into a wolf, is he?"

"No, sweetheart. I think there's just a part of that man that's closer to beast than the rest of us."

Kharrn lowered the ax and looked over at Tom and Hanna, He said, "Are you two all right?"

"About as good as can be expected, hoss. We need to get Hanna out of this storm and get you to a doctor."

"I've had worse," Kharrn said.

"He has," Crowley said, slowly coming to a seated position. "Pulled three arrows out of him at the siege of Byzantium when the Athenians came over the walls."

"What is he saying?" Hanna said.

Kharrn said, "He's raving. But he'll be all right soon. The man's damn hard to kill."

"I'm all right too if anyone is interested," Slate said, rising somewhat unsteadily to his feet. Tom looked over at the pale man. He'd finally lost his hat.

Tom said, "Are all the werewolves dead?"

Kharrn said, "Dead or freed from their curse. Crowley saw to that. We need to see to that girl Crowley was wrestling. Maybe we can catch one or two of the horses."

Tom held onto Hanna and part of him considered how much he would do to protect Hanna and compared that notion with how far Parker had gone to make a family. Would he have gone that far? He could not say and did not want to contemplate the thought for long.

Crowley took off his coat and draped it over the shoulders of the pale woman he'd somehow pulled from inside the werewolf. Had he rescued her? Had he condemned her to a life as a human? Again, Tom was not sure he wanted to know.

They gathered together and turned back toward the town in the growing snowstorm. There was a long journey ahead of them and the sun was hours away.

# Bonus Content:
# Where Did We Go Wrong?

"Why won't you even speak to me, Jonathan?" Her voice rang in his ears and Crowley did his best to ignore her. It wasn't easy. She was persistent.

The cold air bit at his exposed skin and Crowley looked from his perspective atop a four-story apartment building toward the home of his target. The woman inside that building had, according to the people he'd persuaded to talk to him, been dabbling in the sort of sorcery that never goes right.

Joan's voice came from ever closer, the whining note buzzing like a fly next to his left ear. "Jonathan, I know we were never married or anything, but we had fun, didn't we?" He closed his eyes. Yes, they'd had fun.

"Joanie, honey, you should just stop while you're ahead, okay? This isn't going to go the way you want it to, and I'm a little busy right now."

"You know I hate it when you call me Joanie. Makes me sound like I'm twelve." That petulant tone again. Pouty and annoyed and at the same time playful. One night together. It had been a long time ago. Still, she thought that meant something.

"At least you're not ignoring me anymore." He felt the pressure of her fingers on his left shoulder. Jonathan Crowley opened his eyes just in time to see his target across the street opening the leather satchel that contained the book she'd managed to steal from the Boston Occult Archives. The name sounded so formal but the place was little more than a used and new bookstore specializing in tarot readings, Wiccan books and printed paranormal accounts of every type.

He'd actually gone to the store because they had a copy of his *Crowley's Compendium of Exotic Botanicals, 1819 Edition,* a book that was absent from his library. He intended to buy it. They had it on hold.

The damned fools held that one in a lock box. The manuscript that Lianna Potter had in her apartment? That shouldn't have ever made it to their store. Books like that were best destroyed, or if that was not possible, held in a place where no one would ever find them. Like his library.

The Potter woman was carefully laying out the summoning ring that would allow her to summon a demon.

"Jonathan, you're making me angry now. Look at me!"

He looked, and sighed.

She'd been so beautiful once. Bright eyes, a lovely face, and hair he still remembered holding in his hands and smelling as they made love. It was a rare thing for him to be with anyone. A long life means endless chances for regret.

They had not parted company on good terms. She wanted more than he could offer and the names she called him would have ended in a severe beating if she had been someone he felt close enough to for the words to actually hurt.

That was the thing with casual sex. No hard feelings and no looking back.

Now and then the past came to haunt a foolish man despite that philosophy.

So beautiful once, but death was not kind. Her body was long gone. Buried or cremated he had no idea, but her spirit remained, rotting and furious. Her once voluptuous form was desiccated. Her hair had fallen out in heavy patches, leaving bald, rotted bone to remind him of the temple and scalp he'd kissed feverishly. Her breasts, along with most of her internal organs, were gone, lost in a cavernous shadow.

Her eyes were glimmering lights in the sockets of her mildewed face.

"How did you die, Joanie?"

"I—I can't remember."

"Why are you still here, Joanie?"

"Because I love you, baby?" Her voice was a simpering mess and he hated it. Hated the memory of her baby talk after their romp in the dump of a hotel that she and her brother had managed. He remembered her brother, too. How angry he'd been when he called to make accusations.

Hard to remember, it had been a long time ago, but it was possible Crowley and laughed at the man before he killed the phone call.

Really, it was best not to get involved with people. It always went wrong.

"Joanie, honey, if you leave now I can pretend this never happened. For old times' sake."

"Jonathan, baby, come with me. Be with me. We could have so much fun."

Across the street the Potter woman was standing up now, naked and dancing. Her windows were open. How was it that she didn't think to pull the drapes or do anything at all to protect the summoning circle she had made out of little more than salt and a few herbs?

If the twerp who'd owned the bookstore hadn't asked for help, Crowley could have done nothing from where he was. He'd been invited. That made all the difference.

30 yards away, across the street and a story higher than the Potter woman, Crowley saw the air shimmer and distort where the demon was starting to manifest. Did the lady want riches? Revenge? True love to notice her? Did she want to bring back a loved one or, god forbid, a favorite pet? Crowley did not know and did not care.

"Johnny…"

Okay, that did it. No one called him Johnny.

"Remember what I do for a living, Joanie?"

The ruin of Joan's face twisted into a frown of concentration. "Something to do with monsters?"

"Yep. I hunt them. That includes ghosts."

"What's that got to do with me?"

More the pity. She wasn't even aware she was dead.

"Everything." His hand reached out and grabbed at her spectral flesh. He should have slipped right through, but there were dozens of incantations to let him touch a ghost and hundreds that involved exorcising them. This time around, a little something different.

He folded the energies of the dead thing that had once been his lover into a knot of fury. What had been was in the past, but what remained had its uses. If he were a kind man he would have sent her to her final reward. Sometimes that might mean heaven, he had no real idea. He had never been allowed to see the joys of the afterlife except as an unwanted visitor.

Heaven? No idea. Hell? Oh yes, several of them and on numerous occasions.

His pitching arm was just fine. The essence of Joanie shot across the street like a hardball aimed at the batter's face.

She screamed as she ripped through the air and screamed louder still when her spectral energies blew through the lines of salt meant to protect the Potter woman from what she was trying to haul into this world.

The salt line broke.

Joanie shrieked in agony.

The half-formed demon roared out laughter as it drew Joanie to it and then reached out with black, burning hands to pull Lianna Potter to its distorted, half-shaped chest.

The air echoed with screams and laughter alike as the shapes all collapsed in on themselves and were pulled into whatever Hell Potter and been dealing with.

Crowley took the stairs on the way down. He had a book to collect. For a moment he felt bad about Joanie (Not Lianna Potter. She had done that to herself.) and he sighed, remembering what they'd been to each other for a few short hours.

# About the Author

JAMES A. MOORE authored more than forty novels. The first decades of his career focused on his love for horror, as seen in many novels including the critically acclaimed *Fireworks, Under the Overtree, Blood Red,* and the Serenity Falls trilogy. Later, Jim earned a reputation as the "prince of grimdark fantasy" with his hugely popular Seven Forges series as well as the Tides of War trilogy. The author loved collaborating with other writers, most frequently with Christopher Golden on the Bloodstained Worlds trilogy and with Charles R. Rutledge on the Griffin & Price series, among others. Nominated for the Bram Stoker Award twice, Moore won the Shirley Jackson Award for co-editing *The Twisted Book of Shadows*. He first came to prominence as one of the principal world-builders involved in the World of Darkness from White Wolf Games, most famously Vampire: The Masquerade and Werewolf: The Apocalypse. At the time of his passing, Moore left behind one completed solo fantasy novel, as well as completed collaborations with Charles R. Rutledge and Mary SanGiovanni. Plans are afoot to bring those to readers soon.

## Bibliography

### NOVELS

### The Black Stone Bay Series
Blood Red (with "Blood Tide"
Blood Harvest
Bloodlines

### The Bloodstained Series (w/Christopher Golden)
Bloodstained Oz
Bloodstained Wonderland
Bloodstained Neverland

**The Chris Corin Series**
Possessions
Newbies
Rabid Growth

**The Chronicles of Jonathan Crowley**
Under the Overtree
Writ in Blood: Serenity Falls, Book One
The Pack: Serenity Falls, Book Two
Dark Carnival: Serenity Falls, Book Three
Cherry Hill
Smile No More
Boomtown
One Bad Week
Where the Sun Goes to Die

**The Griffin & Price Series (w/Charles Rutledge)**
Blind Shadows
Congregations of the Dead
A Hell Within

**The Seven Forges Series**
Seven Forges
The Blasted Lands
City of Wonders
The Silent Army
The Godless
The War Born

**The Subject Seven Series**
Subject Seven
Run

**The Tides of War Series**
The Last Sacrifice
Fallen Gods
Gates of the Dead

**Standalone Novels**
Deeper
Fireworks
Harvest Moon
The Haunted Forest Tour (w/ Jeff Strand)

**NOVELLAS**
Dear Diary: Run Like Hell
Homestead
The Wild Hunt

**SHORT STORY COLLECTIONS**
Slices
This is Halloween

Curious about other Crossroad Press books? Stop by our website:
http://crossroadpress.com
We offer quality writing
in digital, audio, and print formats.

Subscribe to our newsletter on the website homepage and receive a free
eBook.

www.ingramcontent.com/pod-product-compliance
Lightning Source LLC
Chambersburg PA
CBHW022020170626
46808CB00003B/1000